'GIEREK!'

Hearing his name, t[...]
around and saw the [...]
officer coming through the connecting
door. Alarm flooded through him, but
his snarl was as much due to fear as
savagery. For all that, he was ready to
defend himself with all the courage of a
cornered rat.

Gierek shrieked, bringing up the Colt
and starting to fire, 'I'll kill you!'

Three bullets hissed by Jack Tragg's head
in rapid succession, going through the
door. Unlike the radical, he had kept
count of how many times the pistol had
been fired. Four bullets had already
entered the garage, and, according to the
report he was given on his arrival, three
more had been expended on Route 228.
Which meant the weapon, having a fully
loaded capacity of seven rounds in the
magazine and, possibly, an eighth in the
chamber, had been recharged since
Gierek entered the house.

More than once, in fact!

Having noticed the discarded magazine
lying where it had fallen on the floor, the
sheriff realized that the radical was able
to continue firing at least four and
perhaps five more times!

THE GENTLE GIANT
SET A-FOOT
THE LAW OF THE GUN
THE PEACEMAKERS
TO ARMS! TO ARMS! IN DIXIE!
HELL IN THE PALO DURO
GO BACK TO HELL
THE SOUTH WILL RISE AGAIN
THE QUEST FOR BOWIE'S BLADE
BEGUINAGE
BEGUINAGE IS DEAD!
MASTER OF TRIGGERNOMETRY
THE RUSHERS
THE FORTUNE HUNTERS

The Floating Outfit series, cont'd.

RIO GUNS
GUN WIZARD
THE TEXAN
OLD MOCCASINS ON THE TRAIL
THE RIO HONDO KID
WACO'S DEBT
THE HARD RIDERS
THE FLOATING OUTFIT
APACHE RAMPAGE
THE RIO HONDO WAR
THE MAN FROM TEXAS
GUNSMOKE THUNDER
THE SMALL TEXAN
THE TOWN TAMERS
RETURN TO BACKSIGHT
TERROR VALLEY
GUNS IN THE NIGHT

Waco series

WACO'S BADGE
SAGEBRUSH SLEUTH
ARIZONA RANGER
WACO RIDES IN
THE DRIFTER
DOC LEROY, M.D.
HOUND DOG MAN

Calamity Jane series

CALAMITY, MARK AND BELLE
COLD DECK, HOT LEAD
THE BULL WHIP BREED
TROUBLE TRAIL
THE COW THIEVES
CALAMITY SPELLS TROUBLE

WHITE STALLION, RED MARE
THE REMITTANCE KID
THE WHIP AND THE WAR LANCE
THE BIG HUNT

Alvin Dustine 'Cap' Fog series

YOU'RE A TEXAS RANGER, ALVIN FOG
RAPIDO CLINT
THE JUSTICE OF COMPANY 'Z'
'CAP' FOG, TEXAS RANGER, MEET MR. J.G. REEDER

The Rockabye County series

THE SIXTEEN DOLLAR SHOOTER
THE SHERIFF OF ROCKABYE COUNTY
THE PROFESSIONAL KILLERS
THE ¼ SECOND DRAW
THE DEPUTIES
POINT OF CONTACT
THE OWLHOOT
RUN FOR THE BORDER
BAD *HOMBRE*

James Allenvale 'Bunduki' Gunn series

BUNDUKI
BUNDUKI AND DAWN
SACRIFICE FOR THE QUAGGA GOD
FEARLESS MASTER OF THE JUNGLE

Miscellaneous titles

J.T.'S HUNDREDTH
J.T.'S LADIES
SLAUGHTER'S WAY
TWO MILES TO THE BORDER
SLIP GUN
BLONDE GENIUS (*written in collaboration with Peter Clawson*)
Awaiting publication by Corgi Books

The Lawmen of Rockabye County

J.T. Edson

CORGI BOOKS
A DIVISION OF TRANSWORLD PUBLISHERS LTD

THE LAWMEN OF ROCKABYE COUNTY

A CORGI BOOK 0 552 12025 0

First publication in Great Britain

PRINTING HISTORY
Corgi edition published 1982

Copyright © J.T. Edson 1982

This book is set in 10/11 English Times

Corgi Books are published by
Transworld Publishers Ltd.,
Century House, 61–63 Uxbridge Road,
Ealing, London W5 5SA

Made and printed in
the United States of America by Offset Paperbacks,
Dallas, Pennyslvania.

For Margery Meadows, her 'Yellow Peril',
camera and the flash gun which never
works in Melton Mowbray.

Author's note

To save our 'old hands' from repetition and for the benefit
of all new readers, we have given details of the careers and
special qualifications of Woman Deputy Alice Fayde and
Deputy Sheriff Bradford 'Brad' Counter, also how the
'rights' of a suspect are read, the main police radio codes
and relevant *Articles of the Texas Penal Code* in the form
of Appendices.

We realize that, in our present 'permissive' society, we
could include the actual profanities uttered by various
people. However, we do not concede that a spurious desire
to create 'realism' is a valid reason for doing so.

Lastly, as we do not conform to the current 'trendy'
pandering to the exponents of the metric system, we will
continue to use ounces, pounds, inches, feet, yards and
miles where weights and distances are quoted. The only
exceptions will be when we are referring to the calibres of
such weapons as the Luger 9mm, which are gauged in
millimetres and not fractions of an inch.

J.T. Edson
Active Member, Western Writers of America,
MELTON MOWBRAY,
Leics.,
England.

Case One
Hostages
Prologue

Jack Tragg, the Sheriff of Rockabye County, Texas, was on his way home after having been engaged upon an essential part of his duties, when he received notification that other peace officers not too far away were in need of his assistance.

To an *aficionado* of the very enjoyable, 'message' free, action-escapism-adventure, cinema and television Western movies made prior to the mid-1960's, such a situation evokes a special image where a sheriff — particular in Texas — is concerned.

Tall, lean yet powerful and sun bronzed, such a sheriff will be walking his rounds — the high heels of his sharp-toed boots thunking purposefully and confidently on a wooden side-walk — or riding the range on a fine horse, afork a low horned, double girthed saddle with a Winchester Model of 1873 rifle in its boot. His attire will be that of a cowhand, or occasionally a professional gambler. Carried on a *buscadero* gunbelt, he will have one, or a matched brace of Colt 'Peacemakers'[1] in contoured fast draw holsters. In addition to being chivalrous and courageous, he is invariably an incorruptible defender of law and order.

1. *Information pertaining to the various types of Colt Model 'P' Single Action Army revolver — as it was designated by the manufacturers — first put on the market in 1873 and which became known to many of those who used it as the 'Peacemaker' can be found in those volumes of the* Floating Outfit *series coming after* THE PEACEMAKERS *in the chronological sequence. J.T.E.*

With a height of six foot one inches, which is fairly tall — even by the standards of the Lone Star State — Jack Tragg was lean yet powerful and, framed by his closely cropped black hair, his ruggedly good looking face was deeply bronzed by the sun. What was more, as is the case with the majority of peace officers throughout the Free World — despite numerous suggestions to the contrary made by the 'liberal' elements of the television and movie industry during the late 1970's and early '80's — he was a courageous, chivalrous and incorruptible defender of law and order.

However, while Jack possessed much of the requisite attire to fit the conventional image of a sheriff in Texas, he rarely wore it except during the holiday period known as 'Frontier Week'. At this time, everybody in Gusher City — seat of Rockabye County — was expected to dress in a similar fashion.[2] He also had several fine horses at his disposal and there were still occasions when he found use for their specialized capabilities. For all that, the majority of travelling about his 'bailiwick' in the performance of his duties was in a 'jeep',[3] a light aircraft, a helicopter, or — as on the evening that the present narrative commences — a car.

As was the case with any efficient jet-age representative of law enforcement, combating criminals who made use of every advantage offered by scientific developments, a modern sheriff in Texas needed to move with the times if he was to carry out his multifarious duties in a successful manner. On the other hand, there were also skills created

2. *How one man was affected by arriving in Gusher City during Frontier Week is told in:* Case Three, 'Walt Haddon's Mistake' *of this volume.* J.T.E.

3. *In this instance, we are using the term 'jeep' to describe any small, four-wheel drive vehicle with the capability of travelling across country and not specifically the famous Willys Truck ¼ ton, 4 × 4,* which was given the name, 'Jeep' — derived from a character in the POPEYE *cartoon series* — by servicemen during World War 11. J.T.E.

by the needs of peace officers in the Old West which were equally necessary in the present day. Chief among these, although the techniques and equipment had been improved, was the ability to handle firearms effectively in defensive or offensive situations.

Having been at the handgun range in the basement of the Department of Public Safety Building, participating in the Night Shoot section of the mandatory qualification course fired monthly by every member of the Sheriff's Office and the municipal Gusher City Police Department, Jack was wearing his khaki uniform. The military style shirt, with a neatly knotted black tie — prevented from flapping by a rhodium plated Randall 'Model 12 Bowie' clip — and bearing the shield shaped insignia of his department on its sleeves, matching slacks and black Russel Birdshooter boots, set off his wiry physique to its best advantage. His black John Bianchi Deluxe Sam Browne belt was embossed with 'basket weave' carving, but did not have a shoulder strap.[4] On its left side were pouches for spare ammunition and a set of handcuffs. At the right, in a high riding 'Border Patrol' pattern holster — open topped and raked to the rear after the design perfected by a senior official of that law enforcement agency, who was also acknowledged as a master of combat pistol shooting[5] — he carried a Smith & Wesson Model 57, .41 Magnum calibre revolver with a four inch

---

4. *Designed at the instigation of General Samuel J. Browne (1824–1901) of the British Army, because he had lost an arm in action and needed extra support when carrying his weapons — a pistol when on horseback and a sword if dismounted — the type of military belt which eventually came to bear his name originally had one or two light shoulder straps running diagonally across the chest from left to right. While the basic 'Sam Browne' belt is still popular for uniform wear with peace officers in the United States, the shoulder straps have now gone out of favour and are seldom used. J.T.E.*
5. *The official in question was Assistant Chief Patrol Inspector William H. 'Bill' Jordan, author of one of the most authoritative books available on the subject of modern gun fighting techniques and equipment,* NO SECOND PLACE WINNER. *J.T.E.*

barrel. On entering the vehicle, he had removed his sand coloured Resistol hat — its low crown also bearing the cloth shield of office — and slipped the wide brim into the arms of the holder attached to the roof.

The dark green Buick sedan, of which Jack was the sole occupant, was his private property. Nevertheless, as every peace officer was considered to be available for duty twenty-four hours a day should the need for his — or her — sevices arise, he had had it fitted with certain items of official equipment. One of the additions was the means by which he could keep in contact with Central Control, the permanently manned radio station at the D.P.S. Building. Operated by civilian staff and members of the G.C.P.D.'s Bureau of Communications, its transmitters were sufficiently powerful to reach almost every part of Rockabye County.

It was via this addition the Sheriff learned of the peace officers in his vicinity requiring assistance!

'Cen-Con to all units on 228, southbound!' announced the voice of the duty dispatcher. 'Cen-Con to all units on 228, southbound! R.P. Three-One-Three, Gusher City South, in pursuit two 1256 suspects in orange Ford Torino! Approach with *extreme* caution! They are armed with automatic weapons! Are believed to have killed twice and have fired upon officers giving chase!'

Although calls of various kinds had been relayed with considerable regularity over the frequency to which the sheriff was tuned, he had paid no more than casual attention as he listened to them. All so far had been with regards to routine matters which could be handled by the officers involved and they did not require any intervention on his part.

The latest message was a *very* different proposition!

Not only were the suspects fleeing after possibly having committed a double murder, hence the reference to the specific *Article* in the *Offenses Against The Person Section* of the *Texas Penal Code* which covered that type of crime, but they had started shooting at the officers who

14

were now in pursuit as the crew of the G.C.P.D. Gusher City South Division's radio patrol car numbered 313.

No other call *ever* received such prompt attention from peace officers as when members of a law enforcement agency — not necessarily their own — were, or had come, under fire!

'S.O. One to Cen-Con!' Jack intoned, having instinctively scooped up the handset of his radio and switched it on.

'Cen-Con by, S.O. One!' the dispatcher responded, knowing from the code letters to whom she was speaking as these were given to whatever means of transport the Sheriff of Rockabye County was currently using.

'Am eight miles southbound along Route 228 and turning back!' Jack advised in his lazy sounding Texas drawl. 'Ten-Four?'

'Roger and out!' the dispatcher confirmed.[6]

Replacing the handset on its hook, the Sheriff glanced in the rear view mirror. Having satisfied himself there was nobody coming from behind, he made a deft U-turn. With this completed, he lifted the red 'gumball' emergency light from the front passenger seat. Reaching through the window as it slid down under the impulsion of its automatic mechanism, he applied the magnetic base of the device to the roof of the Buick and set the light flashing. Flicking the headlights to 'high beam', he switched on the siren which was another official addition to the vehicle. Not until all this was done, giving warning of his coming to any innocent users of the road, did he begin to increase speed and drive through the hilly country south of Gusher City in the opposite direction to that in which he had been travelling.

---

6. *An explanation of the various radio call signs employed by the Rockabye County Department of Public Safety can be found in:* APPENDIX THREE. *J.T.E.*

1 *It might be second time lucky*

'Whee-Doggie, good buddy!' ejaculated Patrolman Thomas Garrity, freely flowing perspiration glistening on his black face, as he concentrated upon guiding the black and white Oldsmobile radio patrol car he was driving around a bend on Route 228 at a much greater speed than he would have considered advisable under less pressing circumstances. 'If those hairy sons-of-bitches don't slow down some, the only way we're going to catch them is should they miss a curve and go over the edge!'

'Should they go over, *amigo*, I'd sooner we didn't keep right on after them,' replied Patrolman Herman Klinger, his accent also that of a native born Texan and its tone augmented by the tense expression on his tanned Germanic features, gazing with grim determination at the swiftly moving orange Ford Torino they were pursuing. He never felt entirely at ease when 'riding shotgun' — as the members of the law enforcement agencies of Rockabye County referred to the officer travelling as passenger during the stresses of a chase at high speed, even with a driver he knew to be as competent as his partner and with whom he had worked for the past six years. Glancing ahead, to where the land fell away in a steep and wooded slope just beyond the edge of the road, he continued, 'Was I asked, I'd say this's the wrong god-damned neck of the deep and piney woods for running races. Let's hope somebody has got road blocks set up not too far along.'

'Yah!' Garrity scoffed, showing no offense at the concern over the way in which the pursuit was being carried

16

out as he knew he would be experiencing similar emotions if the roles of his partner and himself were reversed; for the same reasons and with just as little basis. 'Some folks want *everything* done for them.'

'Why surely so,' Klinger conceded, without taking his attention from the vehicle speeding ahead of them. 'And there's *two* who do sitting in this son-of-a-bitching heap right now!'

Working the Afternoon Watch out of the Gusher City South Division station house,[1] the two dark blue uniformed officers of the Gusher City Police Department had noticed something which aroused their suspicions. A front window of a small delicatessen they were passing was punctured with a familar type of roughly star shaped hole which had not been there when they had passed earlier. Calling in a 'Code Six' (Adam) report to inform Central Control of their intentions, they had left R.P. 313 and entered the building to investigate. Seeing the elderly owner and his wife sprawled on the floor, with injuries indicating they had been shot to death only a few minutes ago, the 'harness bulls' had concluded the code words dispatched by Garrity — suggesting that assistance might be required — was justified. Although there had been no sign of the perpetrators of the crime, sounds from a room at the rear had sent them in that direction with revolvers drawn.

Hearing a powerful engine being started outside as they were approaching the partially open door of the back room, the patrolmen had turned to run towards the front entrance. As they were about to go through, they had seen the orange coloured Ford Torino emerging from an alley at the end of the building. However, before they could do more than deduce both occupants of the vehicle were male, a burst of automatic fire from an Armalite Car 15

---

1. *Information regarding the hours worked respectively on the 'two' and 'four' watch rotas by different branches of the law enforcement agencies in Rockabye County is to be found in:* APPENDIX ONE. J.T.E.

S.M.G. 'Commando' carbine, in the hands of the passenger, had compelled them to withdraw.

Sprinting to their Oldsmobile as soon as it was safe to do so, the patrolmen had boarded to give chase. Being slightly the faster runner, Garrity had gone around to act as driver. While Klinger was informing Central Control of what they had discovered in the delicatessen and their present activities, his partner had put the red light and siren into operation and started the vehicle moving. Unfortunately, swiftly as they had acted, the rapidly departing Torino carrying the 'suspects' had already built up a lead by the time they were in motion.

Despite knowing he was permitted under *Article 791, Offenses Against Public Property & Economy* of the *Texas Penal Code* — which stipulated that authorized vehicles were allowed to exceed legal speed limits when *'responding to an emergency call, or in pursuit of actual or suspected violators*, Garrity did not allow his feelings over the murdered couple to lead him to behave rashly. The calming influence was not entirely attributable to him also being aware that *Article 6701D, Section 75* of the legal statutes governing the Sovereign State of Texas stated, *'This section shall not operate to relieve the operator of an authorized emergency vehicle from the duty to drive with due regard for the safety of all persons using the highway.'* Having the welfare of the tax paying citizens and their own peace officers in mind, the County Commissioners insisted that the Department of Public Safety attained a very high standard of competence amongst its personnel. Amongst other things, driving ability was taught and the Emergency Vehicle Operations Course, attendance to which was mandatory, stressed the techniques by which the handling of vehicles during pursuit at high speed through built-up areas could be conducted with the greatest safety.

Having been a suburb of the original town prior to the discovery of extensive oil deposits which brought so massive an expansion the word 'City' was justifiable, the

District through which the early stages of the chase took place was not so busy as would have been the case in certain other areas. However, although it had become apparent that the Torino was heading out of town, Garrity had not forgotten his training. Without even thinking about it consciously, he had used his headlights at 'high beam' and, in addition, made use of the white spot 'horse light' with which the Oldsmobile was fitted to help increase visibility. Keeping the right side wheels well clear of the pavement edge, which might be chipped or higher than the shoulder of the street, he had concentrated on handling the car and relied upon his partner to watch for hazards such as pedestrians, curves or other potentially dangerous objects. When the need arose, Klinger gave a warning in a quiet voice regardless of his misgivings over being driven instead of acting as driver.

Following the rules laid down by and instilled through the E.V.O.C., Garrity had guided the speeding Oldsmobile through the streets of Gusher City South without incident. Two more radio patrol cars and an unmarked vehicle crewed by a team of detectives had come from intersections and followed them by the time the city limits were reached. Unfortunately, however, as yet there had been nobody ahead to try and cut off the escape of the fleeing 'suspects'.

Even on the excellent surface of Route 228, his considerable ability as a driver notwithstanding, Garrity had been unable to close the gap between the Oldsmobile and the Torino to any great extent. In spite of this, neither he nor his partner had even thought of trying to halt the 'suspects' by the dramatic Hollywood system of puncturing a tyre with gun fire. Not only was such a method unlikely to prove successful, due to the extremely high standard of accuracy backed by great good luck required to make a hit — particularly with a handgun — under such conditions, it was illegal even when in pursuit of felons who had already demonstrated a willingness to kill. Slight though it might be along the road, which was not busy, there was always the danger of a bullet which missed the intended target ricocheting and killing some innocent person in the vicinity.

Although the two patrolmen had reconciled themselves to continuing the chase until the 'suspects' could be halted by road blocks established somewhere ahead, as Klinger had commented, Route 228 was now traversing an area which did not induce peace of mind while involved in a chase at high speed. It was winding along the side of a steep hill, with a sheer drop off at one side and a slope rising from the other. While the moon was full, this proved a mixed blessing. For some of the time, the road ahead was illuminated with complete clarity. However, turning a blind bend could suddenly bring the Oldsmobile into black shadows which reduced visibility in an unnerving fashion. Fortunately, the few vehicles which had been overtaken or were approaching had heeded the 'Code Three' warning of the flashing red lights and wailing sirens employed by all the pursuing cars and, having drawn to the extreme edge of the road, had halted until the potential menace had passed by.

'Hey!' Garrity barked, as turning a curve brought the Torino into view something over a quarter of a mile ahead. 'Aren't they slowing down?'

'It looks that way, *amigo*,' Klinger replied and, without the need to think of what he was doing, reached for the twelve gauge Remington Model 870P 'Police Gun'[2] in the rack attached to the ceiling above the front seat of the Oldsmobile. 'I wonder why?'

The question went unanswered!

Not only was the Torino slowing down, it swerved at an angle across the road and came to a halt facing towards the upwards incline. Instantly, its doors flew open and the two occupants sprang out. As they had stopped in an area of bright moonlight, they were exposed to the gaze of the

---

2. *'Police Gun'; for an explanation of the term, see:* Footnote 7, APPENDIX ONE. *J.T.E.*

patrolmen with sufficient clarity for their appearances to be studied and remembered.

Each 'suspect' was tall, lean and would have been termed 'Caucasian' in a description put out by Central Control.[3] Respectively a blond and dark brunette, their hair was shoulder long and each had a beard sufficiently bushy to conceal the majority of his features. They had on loose fitting, collarless, multi-hued shirts which hung outside ragged, faded and much patched Levi's trousers, with tennis sneakers on their feet. Two crossed bandoleers of ammunition were suspended over the shoulders of the blond and he was carrying the automatic carbine. Although the brunette emerged from behind the steering wheel of the Torino with empty hands, he snatched a Colt Government Model of 1911 .45 automatic pistol from the belt — to which was attached a pouch with four spare magazines — around his waist as soon as he was clear of the vehicle.

What happened next established beyond any doubt that the fugitives had not stopped with the intention of surrendering peaceably!

Not that either of the patrolmen had believed such would prove the case!

Snapping the butt of the Armalite to his right shoulder, with the speed of long practice, the blond took rapid aim and opened fire. Almost at the same moment, while running around the front of the Torino, the brunette pointed the automatic pistol behind him at shoulder level and squeezed off three shots. His efforts were, of necessity, less effective than those of his companion.

While the heavier rounds from the Colt went harmlessly into the air, four of the .223 calibre bullets from the carbine struck the windshield of the Oldsmobile. The glass crumpled and turned opaque as, fortunately passing

3. 'Caucasian'; in this context, a member of the white-skinned division of the human race: so called because of a skull found in the Caucasus region, which was taken as establishing the type. J.T.E.

between the occupants, the lead burst through at high velocity. Instantly, Garrity's instincts took over and guided his actions. It said much for his ability as a driver and the high standard of training provided by the Gusher City Police Department's Bureau of Motor Vehicles that he was not only able to keep the car under control with his vision so impaired, but brought it safely to a stop.

'Are you all right, Joe?' Klinger asked, having been protected against the effects of the sudden deceleration by his seat belt — the use of which was mandatory for occupants of official vehicles in Rockabye County — the timbre of solicitude in his voice a marked contrast to his earlier tone.

'Sure am,' the big black patrolman replied, also having been protected by his seat belt. 'How about you?'

'They missed me clean,' Klinger claimed, stabbing a finger at the quick-release catch to free himself from the seat belt. 'Watch how you get out, though. It might be second time lucky!'

'You do the same, *amigo*!' Garrity advised, also liberating himself. 'God damn it, there must be an *easier* way of making a living!'

'You find the sucker,' Klinger growled, unfastening his door. 'Then let me know and *I'll* take it!'

Swiftly as the two patrolmen quit the vehicle, the fugitives had moved even faster. Neither was anywhere to be seen by the time Garrity and Klinger were standing on the road. Nor, with the various sounds originating from their rear, could they hear anything to suggest in which direction the pair of 'suspects' had departed.

In spite of the squealing of brakes being applied which caused tyres to protest against the sudden restriction upon their movements, the other r.p.'s and the car carrying the detectives having been following at a distance which offered a sensible margin of safety, were all able to halt without any collisions. Leaving their respective vehicles, armed with a variety of weapons, the six peace officers advanced cautiously towards R.P. 313. Only one of the arrivals in the unmarked vehicles was a man, but the uniformed officers were not in the least perturbed by discovering this to be the case.

Big, buxom, black-haired, Woman Detective Rachel Winters looked like a matronly Jewish housewife of moderate means and was a very competent peace officer. Having handed her partner, Detective David Bulpin, the short High Standard Model 10 Series A Police Shotgun she had brought from their car, she drew the snub-nosed Colt Diamondback revolver from her bulky Pete Ludwig shoulder bag. It was no mere affectation. If the need arose, qualifying as 'Marksman', she could hold up her end in a gun fight.

'Where'd they go, gents?' Bulpin asked, his appointment as detective giving him a rank equivalent to a sergeant of the Patrol Bureau and, in the absence of anybody with a greater seniority, putting him in command of the assembled peace officers.

'I don't know,' Garrity replied, after his partner had glanced in his direction. 'The bastard with the Armalite Car bust the windshield in our faces and we couldn't see which way they lit out.'

'They've headed upwards, not down, I'd say,' Klinger supplemented, riding shotgun having allowed him to maintain a better surveillance of the fugitives as he had not needed to devote any of his attention to driving. 'At least, that's the way the son-of-a-bitch who was at the wheel took off when they left their heap.'

'Looks like it falls off pretty near straight down on the other side, anyways,' commented one of the patrolmen from the black and white 'back up' cars. 'But why the hell did they stop *here*?'

'Out of gas, maybe?' Bulpin guessed, correctly as was established by a subsequent examination of the Torino. Turning his gaze in the direction suggested by Klinger, he listened for a moment to the rattle of loose stones and dirt being dislodged by the fugitives as they were making their ascent and went on, 'They're going *up*, that's for sure.'

'You know something, gents?' Rachel inquired, her voice a deep contralto and somewhat husky. 'Those *momzers* aren't trying to make it *easy* for us!'

'That's a big affirmatory they aren't,' Bulpin seconded, glancing at the slope again. 'Bring all the cars up, Rachel, gents. Keep the headlights on full and we'll see happen we can pick them out that way.'

The order was carried out quickly, but with little positive effect!

In fact, the response to the suggestion was less than satisfactory!

Even with the vehicles halted so they were facing straight across the width of the road, their combined headlights could only illuminate the bottom dozen or so feet of the hillside. Nor was the attempt made by Rachel to improve the situation any more productive. Returning her revolver to its holster in the shoulder bag, she collected the spotlight carried in the unmarked car. When she switched it on and, keeping herself concealed as far as possible behind the vehicle, started to sweep its powerful beam methodically back and forth, the Armalite spluttered. A startled and profane exclamation burst from her as the spotlight, its glass and bulb disintegrated by a bullet, was sent flying from her grasp.

Four shotguns of various kinds and three revolvers barked, being aimed at the flashes from the automatic weapon of the blond haired fugitive. However, there was no indication that any of the charges set loose had achieved their intended purpose.

'Did he get you, Rachel?' Bulpin asked worriedly, lowering the High Standard.

'Knocked the light out of my hand is all,' the woman detective replied, shaking and working her stinging fingers. 'Did you get him?'

'I wouldn't want to chance saying "yes" to that,' Bulpin assessed. 'If we hit him, he surely kept quiet about it unless we killed him outright.'

'Sounds like we didn't get him, they're moving again,'

24

Garrity commented, scanning the slope as the noise of the ascent through the darkness was resumed. 'But where do those yoyos think they're headed?'

'Yeah,' Klinger seconded. 'There's nothing but open range once they get over the ridge unless they figure to cut back to the road here further along.'

'There *is* though, by god!' Bulpin ejaculated, also looking upwards. 'Unless I'm mistaken, there's a turn off around the next bend and it leads up to one of those high-rent Hillside Estates. Some of the houses must be right above us!'

'Hell's fires, yes!' Klinger spat out. 'If they should get into one of them, those god-damned yoyos could make a stand, or maybe take hostages.'

'Then we'd better get up that turn off *muy pronto*!' Rachel declared, glancing at the car in which she and her partner had arrived. 'Maybe we can reach the houses before they can get to one.'

'There's not a god-damned chance of that,' Bulpin replied savagely. 'I've worked this area. The turn off winds back and forth for half a mile or more before it gets up to that level and it's not a road you can run over at speed.'

'Like I said,' Rachel breathed. 'Those *momzers* aren't trying to make things any too easy for us!'

'And, like *I* said, you've got a big affirmatory on *that*!' the male detective answered. Then, after telling the assembled peace officers to "get set", he cupped his hands around his mouth and raised his voice to a stentorian bellow, 'Hey, you two up there. Can you hear me?'

'We hear you, you "mother-something" Fascist pig!'[4] a voice with a close to whining Mid-West accent screamed from the blackness of the slope. 'What do you want?'

'Give it up and come back down here!' Bulpin advised. 'You can't get away on foot!'

This time, the answer was not verbal!

---

4. *See second paragraph of our:* AUTHOR'S NOTE. *J.T.E.*

Red flashes burst in rapid succession from the gloom some distance above where the earlier shots had been fired!

Already alert to the possibility of such hostile action, the peace officers had taken the precaution of keeping the vehicles between themselves and the incline. Hearing the response yelled to Bulpin's suggestion of surrender, all but one had begun to crouch down by the time the first bullet struck and ricocheted from the concrete surface.

The exception, Klinger, had remained partially erect in the hope of employing his Remington. Before he could do so, a cry of pain burst from him. Spinning around, the automatic shotgun falling from his hands as they clutched at his chest, he sprawled limply face down on the road.

Echoing the involuntary exclamation which burst from Garrity, Bulpin halted his descent to safety. Reversing his direction just a trifle more swiftly than the remaining pair of patrolmen who were armed in a similar fashion, he thrust the assault weapon he was holding into a firing position. A beam stabbed from the removable flashlight on top of the purpose built shotgun, but he made no attempt to pinpoint the target with its illumination. Instead, he expended four of the two and three-quarter inch long shells from the tubular magazine in spraying their respective loads of nine .32 calibre buckshot balls towards the general area from which the multiple flashes of the carbine had originated. Although the uniformed officers duplicated his actions, apart from a cessation of firing from up the slope, there was nothing to suggest their combined efforts had taken effect.

'Hold it right there, Joe!' Bulpin barked, as Garrity spat out a profanity and began to rise. '*That* isn't the way and you *know* it!'

For a moment, it seemed the big black patrolman would ignore the command!

Then the discipline ingrained by his service with the United States Marines and the G.C.P.D., aided by his common sense, caused Garrity to obey. He realized that, personal feelings notwithstanding, to dash off recklessly in search of revenge for his stricken partner would do nothing to improve the situation. In fact, by rushing into the darkness of the slope, he would seriously restrict the ability of the other peace officers to take action. They would be afraid of inadvertantly hitting him if they opened fire on the fugitives.

'Get on the horn and have an ambulance sent here *muy pronto*!' Bulpin ordered, directing the words at a patrolman who was armed with a revolver. 'Tell Cen-Con we need more help out here, too!'

'Yo!' the uniformed officer replied, making the traditional assent to a command of the United States Cavalry and holstering his weapon.

'I'll see to your partner, Joe,' Rachel offered. 'Check whether his riot gun is still in working order, you might need it.'

'Somebody's already coming,' remarked one of the uniformed officers, a moment later, nodding towards the sound of a siren rapidly drawing nearer from the direction in which the pursuit had been heading. 'Likely one of the sher —!'

'There they are!' yelled another of the patrolmen, gesturing upwards with his Colt Python revolver.

Following the direction indicated, the remaining peace officers saw something which all regarded with considerable misgivings!

Hitherto unnoticed by any of the party on the road, as they were concentrating upon scanning the slope, stood one of the houses to which Bulpin had referred. Its front had been in darkness. Like all the properties on the Hillside Estates developments, providing one had no objections to there being a steep slope of more than a hundred yards in depth separating the front garden by no more than a narrow dirt road, it was a beautiful place. Although it had been unlit previously, apparently the occupants had heard the shooting. Showing what the watching peace officers considered to be a remarkable lack

27

of good sense, somebody inside had switched on the porch light.

The two fugitives showed briefly in the illuminated area!

Before any of the peace officers could even consider whether it would be safe to open fire, much less make any attempt to do so, the long haired pair had crossed the porch and disappeared from view. There was a crash of breaking glass as one of them, probably the blond using the butt of his carbine, smashed either a window or a panel in the front door. A moment later, a feminine scream of fright rang out.

'And *that* is all we god-damned need!' Bulpin declared bitterly, straightening up. 'They've got themselves some hostages. Which, happen they figure on staying put, we'll have hell's own time and trouble smoking them out!'

2   Institute 'Operation Gob-Stopper'

'Well now, Rachel, gentlemen,' Jack Tragg said pensively, gazing up the slope. 'I'd say we've got ourselves something of a *problem*. We've got to find ourselves some way of smoking those yoyos out of there and without putting whoever else's inside at risk.'

Although all the officers who were present so far belonged to the Gusher City Police Department, the Sheriff of Rockabye County had automatically assumed control over the operation when he arrived on the scene. Not only was he senior in rank to all of them, but technically they were now well beyond the limits of the city and, therefore, within the area of his jurisdiction.

'It's not going to be easy, sir,' Detective David Bulpin claimed, despite knowing that the same conclusion would already have occurred to the newcomer. But he had acquired a piece of information which he considered gave added confirmation to his summation. 'Particularly if those yoyos are who I reckon they might be.'

'Who's that, Dave?' Jack inquired, without turning his attention from the building which — the porch light having been switched off just prior to his arrival — was once again in darkness.

'Going by that Armalite Commando carbine and the descriptions of them that Patrolman Garrity's given to me, the blond's Richard Cleverly and the brunette's Edward Gierek,' Bulpin supplied, having elicited the details partly to distract the thoughts of the big black 'harness bull' from his seriously wounded partner who was being given first aid and what comfort was possible by Woman Detective Rachel Winters prior to the arrival of more qualified medical aid. 'They're a couple of radical activists who're wanted out of Houston on 1151 and 1256 raps.'

'Just a couple of good old Communist boys fighting against the evils of the Capitalist Establishment, huh?' Jack drawled sardonically.

'Why sure,' the detective agreed. 'Except, although it's all right for *them* to label *us* "Fascists", we're doing a McCarthy witch hunt should we say they're Commies. Only I thought their kind were only supposed to rob the rich, like good old Robin Hood, and the Moreno family at the delicatessen were anything but rich.'

'I've never known any of those stinking crud who wouldn't rob a blind beggar should they need money,' the Sheriff declared and, crossing to his Buick, lifted out the handset of the radio. 'S.O. One to Cen-Con!'

'Cen-Con by!' replied the dispatcher at Central Control.

'Are any S.O. units approaching my ten-twenty?'

'S.O. Six and S.O. Nine on their way!'

'Patch me through to them,' Jack ordered, having already notified the dispatcher that he was at the scene. With contact made, he continued, 'S.O. One to S.O. Six and S.O. Nine. Institute "Operation Gob-Stopper". Ten Four?'

'Roger, S.O. One,' replied the Deputy Sheriff riding shotgun in sheriff's office car Six. 'You've got "Gob-Stopper". Over and out.'

Although they were speeding along Route 228 in response to the instructions given by Central Control, knowing what was required to institute 'Operation Gob-Stopper', the drivers of the two vehicles slowed down. Then, while S.O. Nine halted and reversed until across the road at an angle with its hood pointed towards Gusher City, S.O. Six advanced a short distance to take up a similar position facing in the way they had been travelling. By doing so, they formed a narrow channel through which everybody else coming along the road would be compelled to negotiate slowly unless willing to try smashing through. To cope with the latter contingency, the deputies brought riot guns from their vehicles. Then, leaving the red lights flashing, they stood alongside S.O. Nine to check the identity of anybody travelling southwards along the road and warn them of the danger of going further.

There was, however, more to 'Operation Gob-Stopper' — the name having been selected by Brenda, the English-born wife of Jack Tragg — than appeared upon the surface!

While the media in Rockabye County was less infested by 'liberals' than that of New York, Los Angeles, or San Francisco, two of the interviewers for the local television station were of such a persuasion and the *Gusher City Mirror* employed no other kind of journalists. Aware of their close to paranoid hatred of the Free World's law enforcement agencies and officers, the sheriff had no desire to have any of them on the scene while dealing with a situation involving radical activists. If they should have been monitoring the calls from Central Control the four deputies, having received the appropriate code name, would delay them for as long as possible and allow him to take whatever action he considered necessary without their interference.

'Here we go, gents,' Jack drawled, returning the handset at the conclusion of his message and studying the situation with the eyes and instincts of an exceptionally competent, experienced peace officer.[1] Noticing the hillside rose only about thirty foot above the house, but in the form of an almost sheer cliff, he went on, 'Let's have all the spotlights we've got trained above the house. It's not likely those two yoyos will decide to try some more climb-

---

1. *The family of Sheriff Jack Tragg have had a long tradition for being involved in the enforcement of law and order in Texas. Information regarding three earlier Traggs who served as peace officers can be found in:* SET A-FOOT, BEGUINAGE IS DEAD! *and the various volumes of the* Alvin Dustine 'Cap' Fog *series. J.T.E.*

ing, but I want that area kept illuminated in case they should give it a whirl.'

'I just hope the bastards do *try* it!' stated the youngest of the harness bulls from the back up radio patrol cars, having collected an Armalite M-16 automatic rifle out of the trunk of his team's vehicle to supplement his handgun. Hefting the powerful weapon with grim appreciation and glancing to where Patrolman Herman Klinger was lying, he continued, 'I'll bet neither of them make it to the top!'

'They'll be given every chance to surrender, should they want it that way,' the Sheriff said, looking around and, despite understanding the sentiments of the speaker — even sympathizing with them to a certain degree — his voice held a warning. Then, satisfied the point he had made had been taken by all the other peace officers, he returned his attention to the task in hand. 'We'll try to talk them out first.'

'They won't come,' Bulpin guessed and the patrolman rumbled concurrence with his point of view.

'Likely not,' Jack admitted. 'But doing it will give us more time to try and figure out a way to get to them when they don't. As I see it, our best chance would be to get above the house and come down on to the roof.'

'It'll be one hell of a rough climb, was I asked,' Bulpin commented wryly, raising his gaze to the building. 'Looks to me like we'll have to go up off to one side and out of their range of vision, then work along the face of the cliff until we're over the house. If one of them happens to look out of a window and spots us hanging on to it, I don't reckon we'll be around long enough to retire on pension.'

'There's nothing more certain than *that*, Dave,' the Sheriff conceded, noticing with approval how the detective had assumed — being one of the senior officers present — he would take part in the attempt. 'So we'll give *talking* them out a whirl first. If that doesn't work, we'll have to do it the hard way.'

'Go get the "Super Hailer" from the trunk of our heap,' Bulpin told the youngest of the patrolmen. Then, while the

32

order was being obeyed, he returned his attention to Jack. 'Shall we use your Buick or our heap to go up there?'

'Neither,' the Sheriff replied. 'Those yoyos will know we wouldn't let any civilians through and hearing a car go by would warn them we could be up to something.'

'Then we'll have to climb the slope like they did,' the detective estimated. 'Well, if they could, I reckon there's no doubt we can.'

'Here you are, sir,' announced the youngest harness bull, offering the Sheriff the Audio Equipment Company Model S-183 'Super Hailer' megaphone he had been sent to collect from the unmarked car used by the detectives.

'*You* use it, Dave!' Jack instructed. 'Let them know that we've made them, but don't say *I'm* here.'

'Yo!' assented the detective, being aware of the reason for the latter part of the order. Lifting the megaphone, he switched it on and said, 'Richard Cleverly! Edward Gierek!'

As Bulpin was speaking the spotlights, which were also standard equipment in the radio patrol cars, were brought into action. With the words booming out and echoing eerily, the three powerful beams were directed upwards. As the Sheriff had instructed, they were directed at the sheer cliff face beyond rather than at the building.

The megaphone was a top quality, self contained unit. Charged with ten standard 'D' size flashlight batteries, which had only recently been renewed, it could project verbal messages in an intelligible fashion to distant listeners even when there was a high level of noise — such as might be encountered from a rowdy crowd, or a hostile mob — interfering. In the silence of the night, despite the doors and windows being closed, it would therefore be heard by the occupants of the house with perfect clarity.

Gazing upwards, the Sheriff was impressed and satisfied by the note of grim inexorability with which Bulpin had pronounced the names. It suggested, as was indeed the case, that the peace officers were in grim and deadly earnest. Jack wondered how the two cornered fugitives felt as they looked down into the glaring lights and listened to the implication — hopefully correct — reverberating across the countryside that their identities were known to the lawmen on the road. From up there, even if they could not hear the sirens, they might be able to see other units speeding to the scene, bringing well armed reinforcements to strengthen the party already arrayed against them.

'You're completely hemmed in!' the greatly magnified voice of the detective boomed on remorselessly. 'Why drag it out when you know you can't hope to beat it in the long run?' After a short pause, to allow the import of the words to strike home, he went on, 'You have five minutes to come out with your hands in the air. If you don't, we'll be coming in after you. How about it?'

There was no immediate reply from above!

One minute dragged by!

Then two!

And three!

Four more official cars of various kinds arrived, followed by an ambulance from the Central Receiving Hospital in Gusher City carrying an intern and a team of paramedics.

One of the newcomers, the Watch Commander of Gusher City South Division, informed the sheriff that 'Operation Gob-Stopper' was working and a 'liberal' newspaperman from the *Gusher City Mirror* was being delayed by the deputies.

Still more spotlights were switched on, now bathing the house as well as the cliff beyond in a glow of brilliant whiteness. However, on the orders of the sheriff, the area to either side of the building was deliberately left in darkness and this was even blacker as a result of the glare.

Two more minutes crept away!

'Cleverly! Gierek!' the amplified voice of Bulpin warned, in response to a nod from Jack. 'Your time's run out. What is it to be?'

The porch light was switched on!

Every peace officer who possessed a weapon with sufficient range for it to be effective gripped it more tightly and began to align its sights!

Suddenly, crossing the porch and violently, waving a white handkerchief, a single figure appeared!

'That's not either of them!' Garrity shouted urgently.

'All officers!' the detective barked into the microphone, having made a similar estimation and needing no instructions from either of his superiors on what to do. 'All officers, hold your fire. Repeat, *hold* your fire!'

Crossing the front garden and coming through the gate in the picket fence, the man from the house turned along the narrow road which wound down the hillside to join Route 228. It descended at a gradual angle for a short way, reversed itself in a hairpin bend, ran some distance in the opposite direction and turned back once more. Continuing to signal his harmless intentions vigorously with the handkerchief, he disappeared from view after the second bend. Wanting to hear what he had to say as quickly as possible, the sheriff dispatched one of the newly arrived radio patrol cars to fetch him. When he arrived, he proved to be shortish, plump, about fifty years of age and with a face which normally would have been jovial. He was bare headed, in his shirt sleeves and had moccasins on his feet.

'Those two god-damned, stinking bastards!' the man gasped, with a Texas accent — being in such poor physical condition he was still somewhat short of breath in spite of having completed the remainder of the journey from the house in the car. 'They burst in on us waving guns and saying they'd kill us, the long haired sons-of-bitches!'

'We saw them,' Jack replied, walking forward accompanied by the uniformed Commander. 'But there was no way we could stop them from down here without shooting and we didn't want to chance doing that without knowing who was in the house.'

'I can see that, Sheriff Tragg,' the man declared. 'And thank god you're here. They've sent me —!'

'Do you mind telling us your name, please, sir?' Jack interrupted, wanting to give the speaker time to recover his wits fully.

'Lacey,' the man supplied. 'Oliver Lacey. I own Lacey's Video Services.'

'This is Captain Bellamy of Gusher City South,' the Sheriff introduced. 'And that's your place up there?'

'Sure.'

'Is your family in the house?'

'No!'

'*No*?' Jack queried, remembering the reference to 'us' and deducing from the single word response that whoever was present might not be considered acceptable company.

'Not my *family*,' Lacey corrected. 'They're away on vacation, thank god!'

'But you weren't alone?' the sheriff prompted.

'Well, I —!' the man began, darting a worried glance at the peace officers who were standing around. 'That is —!'

'Maybe we'd best go talk about it in my car?' Jack suggested, concluding his suppositions were correct. 'Just you, Captain Bellamy and myself.

'I — I'd prefer it that way,' Lacey admitted, glancing at the tall, slim, middle-aged man in the uniform of a senior officer in the Gusher City Police Department and thinking that there did not appear to be any inter-departmental hostility between the members of the municipal and county law enforcement agencies, despite almost every current television 'cop' series implying such was invariably the case. 'Thank you.'

'Who do you have up there?' Jack inquired, as soon as the privacy he had suggested was attained.

'A — A couple of girls,' Lacey confessed, looking in embarassment from one peace officer to the other as they occupied the seat in front of him. 'Not *minors*, but — well, I suppose you'd call them "hookers", although I hadn't got them at the house to —!'

'And there were only the *three* of you?' Captain Henry Bellamy inquired.

'Yes,' Lacey confirmed, looking far from at ease about the information he was divulging. 'You see there's this business associate of mine I'm trying to set up a big deal with and, as we're both into apartment house wres —!'

'He didn't show?' the Sheriff guessed, as the explanation trailed off uncompleted.

'No,' the plump man replied and, although he felt sure wrong conclusions were being drawn, he decided against telling the real reason for the two prostitutes being invited.[2] Instead, he went on, 'Would you believe, of all things, he'd caught himself a damned bad attack of diarrhoea and couldn't make it?'

'It happens,' Jack smiled, being more interested in the two radicals than learning why Lacey had the women on the premises.

'Thank god it did this time!' the man declared vehemently. 'Having those two bushy haired bastards burst in on us while he was visiting with me wouldn't have done anything to improve my chances.'

'Likely,' the Sheriff drawled with a grin of genuine sympathy. 'Why'd they let *you* come down here, Mr. Lacey?'

'It scared the crap out of them when they heard you know who they are,' the man answered. 'So they've sent me down to tell you their terms.'

'Which are?' Jack asked, although he could have made an accurate guess.

'They said they're going to take my car, come down and go to Gusher City Airport, where you're to have an aircraft with enough fuel aboard to fly them direct to Cuba,' Lacey explained, as the Sheriff had guessed would be the case. 'They said for me to be real sure I warned you they've got the girls and they'll kill both of them if they don't get what they're asking for.'

'They turned *you* loose and hung on to a pair of hookers

2. *A suggestion of why the two prostitutes were present can be found in:* THE SHERIFF OF ROCKABYE COUNTY. *J.T.E.*

as their hostages?' Bellamy growled and swung a bewildered gaze at the other peace officer. 'God damn it, Jack, that doesn't make any sense!'

'It does to *them*, the way they've got it figured out,' Lacey asserted. 'The blond bastard told me I should warn you how, when word got out that you'd let a couple of *Chicano* girls be killed rather than give way to their demands, the "Party" would have every Hispanic and "support the down-trodden ethnic minorities" freak in Texas rioting on the streets in protest. They were trying to reach those god-damned soft-shell newscasters at the television studio on the telephone when I came out and they're figuring on calling the *Mirror* next to make sure the word gets spread for them. That's what those pinko crud would do, when they hear, and be grateful for the excuse.'

'We've seen it,' Jack admitted sombrely, being all too aware of the way in which the 'liberal' elements used the media to incite racial hatred and tensions for their own ends. 'But there'll be no giving in to them.'

'God damn it!' Lacey protested angrily. 'Those bastards weren't kidding when they said they'd kill the girls. You can't put their lives in danger.'

'You sound as if you care what happens to them.' Bellamy remarked.

'You can bet your god-damned life I care about them!' the plump man almost shouted and there was no doubt his fury was genuine. 'It's on account of *me* that Rosa and Maria are out here tonight and I'll be "somethinged" before I'll let you —!'

'Hold hard there, Mr. Lacey!' the captain requested, raising his right hand in a placatory gesture. 'I'm sorry. Like the Sheriff's wife says, "that was one of those things wot could have been better put". No offense was intended. But are you *certain* in your own mind those yoyos meant what they said?'

'They meant it all right!' Lacey claimed, with complete conviction and showing signs of being mollified by the apology. 'Hell, they reek of pot and I'm willing to bet that's not the hardest thing they're high on. Yes sir, there's no way they're just bluffing.' He shook himself violently, as if to control his churned up emotions, then went on in a less vehement fashion. 'I know the kind of tight this puts you in, Sheriff, Captain. If you give way to them, you've established a precedent that will give encouragement to every other god-damned radical who finds himself on the run from the law. If it wasn't for Maria and Rosa, I'd say go up there and fetch those two hairy sons-of-bitches out any way you have to. Even if you have to burn the house down.'

'Don't worry, Mr. Lacey, keeping the girls from coming to harm is our number one priority,' Jack declared with sincerity, comparing favourably the genuine concern of the portly messenger with the way in which the character of a successful and prosperous businessman — particularly one who had such a pronounced Southern accent — would have been portrayed in the kind of movies and television shows currently being made. 'Have they given you a deadline for getting their answer?'

'I didn't know *you* were here,' Lacey replied. 'So I warned them there was sure to be a delay while the officers contacted somebody in Gusher City with enough authority to give a decision on their demands. The blond wasn't happy about it, but his *amigo* said it would give the folk from the media a chance to get out here and cover them.'

'That *wasn't* why we didn't let them know I was here, but I'm not sorry it made up their minds to accept the delay,' Jack remarked and glanced at Bellamy. 'We'd best start making use of the time we've bought us, Hank.'

'Why sure,' the captain agreed. 'There's a limit to how long your boys can make the "Gob-Stopper" stick.'

'You're not going to give in to them, are you?' Lacey asked, more as a statement than a question.

'You've already said why we *can't*,' Jack reminded, as Bellamy was leaving the Buick. 'And so we're going to take them at the house, where they won't be expecting it.' He raised his hand in a gesture of gentle restraint before

Lacey could speak, then continued, 'No, it won't be a frontal assault, or even by driving up from here.'

'They said they knew you wouldn't let anybody other than cops come up by car,' the businessman claimed. 'You could have some of your men lowered on to the roof from a helicopter — Except they'd hear it overhead and guess what was happening.'

'Which's why doing it that way is out,' the Sheriff asserted. 'So two of us will be going up the slope on foot, along the cliff and on to the roof, then get in from there.'

'*Along* the cliff?' Lacey repeated, staring in a startled fashion at the Sheriff. 'God! That'll be dangerous, even if your men are wearing bulletproof clothing.'

'Which we won't be,' Jack answered. 'Climbing around up there will be difficult enough without being weighted down with protective clothing capable of stopping a bullet from that Armalite carbine.'

'You keep saying, "*us*",' Lacey commented, staring at the tanned face of the man on the front seat. 'Does that mean *you* will be going personally?'

'Of course,' the Sheriff replied, opening the door of the Buick. 'And I'll need to know all you can tell me about the layout of your house.'

A feeling of deep respect welled through the businessman!

Lacey knew the decision to participate had not been reached through a desire to grab any glory which might accrue from a successful rescue attempt!

Nor was it made out of a morbid wish to face danger!

Although he had not expressed the point, Jack Tragg knew his responsibility to those under his command!

A lesser man would have explained why he was taking the risk, rather than endangering the life of a subordinate, but such was not the way of the Sheriff of Rockabye County!

3   I can't promise that I can

'My wife's been bugging me about taking more exercise,' remarked Patrolman Joseph Garrity, standing among the trees at the foot of the steep slope and looking upwards. 'She reckons I'm putting on weight since I've been riding a black and white instead of walking a beat.'

'Wives are like that,' Jack Tragg sympathized with a grin. 'Well, I'd say you're going to have plenty of exercise before we get through.'

'That's for sure,' the burly black harness bull confirmed wryly, running a big hand across his bare head. 'Thing being, I reckon I'd be a whole heap happier was I to have taken up jogging.'

'It's too late to change your mind now,' the Sheriff of Rockabye County warned. 'Let's go before that crapper from the *Mirror* arrives.'

On rejoining the assembled peace officers, after having obtained a very thorough description of the building in which the hostages were being held, and having received from its owner an item which might prove of the greatest value, Jack had quickly explained how he intended to handle the situation. As had been the case with Oliver Lacey, probably even more so, the men of the Gusher City Police Department had understood and appreciated his unspoken motivation. With one exception, they had also wondered who would be the second participant in the far from safe scheme. Before Captain Henry Bellamy could volunteer in his capacity of senior municipal officer present and therefore under a similar obligation to that of

41

the Sheriff, Garrity had stepped forward, glancing to where the ambulance was about to carry away Patrolman Herman Klinger — whose wound was serious, but not definitely terminal — and asked if he could go.

'Do you think you can cut it as a *peace officer* and not just a feller looking to take revenge for a good friend?' Jack had inquired, wanting to have the Gusher City South Watch Commander co-ordinating matters of Route 228.

'Well no, sir, I can't promise that I can,' the black patrolman confessed without any attempt at evasion. 'Hermie and me have been together for too many watches, and tight ones, to let me treat it like a stranger was shot. But I'd feel a whole heap easier in my mind if I could go back and tell him — and our wives — that I'd helped bring those two hairy bastards in.'

'If you'd given me a straight out, "yes", I'd be calling for a volunteer,' Jack had asserted frankly. 'As it is, providing Captain Bellamy doesn't object, I'll be pleased to have you along.'

'I've known Joe ever since he was a rookie,' the Watch Commander had stated, after having studied his subordinate for a moment. 'And I can't think of a better man to have backing you, Jack.'

'Then that's all settled,' the Sheriff had decided. 'All right, Joe, this's how we'll try to play it.'

There had not been time for any too lengthy a discussion. Shortly after Jack had given his consent for Garrity to accompany him, the senior of the deputy sheriffs carrying out 'Operation Gob-Stopper' had radioed a warning that they had run out of excuses for delaying the reporter from the *Gusher City Mirror* and an equally 'liberal' female newscaster from the local television network was also on her way with a two-man crew. Wanting to avoid them discovering he was already on the scene, the Sheriff had given orders for his Buick sedan to be taken along the road and concealed on the turn off below where it might be seen and arouse the suspicions of the fugitives. Then, having completed the arrangements as far as was possible, he and Garrity had set off together.

'Richard Cleverly, Edward Gierek!' Detective David Bulpin called over the "Super Hailer" megaphone. Waiting for a few seconds without receiving any reply, he continued to carry out his instructions. 'Mr. Lacey has told us what you want from us, but there's nobody down here with the authority to deal with you. We've notified the Sheriff and Chief of Police Hagen, but you'll have to wait it out until one or the other arrives.'

Having turned their backs on Route 228 while the names of the fugitives were being called, the Sheriff and Garrity delayed no longer in commencing their ascent. They went carefully, testing every hand- and foothold on the steep incline before trusting their respective full weight upon its support. The reasons for the precautions were threefold. Firstly ascending the slope in the darkness would be far from easy and to loose one's footing could result in an injury. Then, even if it did not injure them, the commotion might be heard by the fugitives. And finally it could alert the 'liberals' from the media that action was being taken to rescue the hostages.

Shortly after the message ended, one of the men in the building answered. Although they could hear his voice, it lacked the volume offered by the megaphone and neither Jack nor the patrolman could make out what was being said. Nor, the going being rendered even more strenuous by the need to avoid making any more noise than was absolutely inescapable, did they offer to discuss what the response from above might have been.

Despite being aware that his companion was in far better physical shape than had been intimated while they were standing at the edge of the road, the sheriff accepted they would not be able to complete the gruelling climb in a single, continuous ascent. Therefore, after they had crossed the narrow access road and reached the point at which the incline became a nearly sheer cliff, they stopped to rest for a while before commencing the most difficult part of the climb.

From their position, the two peace officers could see the house clearly. It was something over a hundred yards to their right and on the same level. Except for the section of the cliff face over which they would have to make their final approach, the whole area was brilliantly illuminated by the spotlights. Even in the glow of the full moon, this formed a darkish strip in contrast with the glare above and below it. However, they concluded the sight was not fully reassuring as they could still make out various details of the near vertical surface in the darkened area. Each appreciated that, if one or other of the fugitives should glance out of any window on the west side of the building, they were unlikely to escape being noticed.

'How do you feel now, Joe?' the Sheriff inquired, *sotto voce*.

'Like I shouldn't *never* have gone against the habits of a lifetime by saying I'd volunteer for something,' Garrity replied, just as quietly. 'I slipped back there and tore a knee out of my pants.'

'Hard luck,' Jack drawled, glancing to make sure the patrolman had not also sustained an injury to his leg. 'Anyways, you can always put in a claim for a replacement due to damage caused in the line of duty and the ''Money-Grubbers'' might let it through.'

'I noticed how you said, ''*might*'' and not ''*will*'',' the black patrolman commented with a grin, being aware of the thoroughness with which the Bureau of Accounts examined every claim for expenses. Then, throwing a quick look at the hole in the right leg of his dark blue uniform trousers, he gave a shrug and went on, 'Oh well, happen I do much more of this kind of healthy exercise, they soon wouldn't have fitted me anyway.'

'I'd sooner *not* be doing any of *this* kind of healthy exercise even the once,' the Sheriff stated. 'You know something, Joe?'

'Depends what, sir.'

'Now we're up close, that god-damned cliff doesn't look any easier to move across than it did from down below.'

'I was wondering whether *you* would notice that. Although, was I asked, I'd be inclined to say it looks even *harder* now we're up here.'

'I hope that wasn't intended as a pun?' Jack asked, having continued to survey the situation whilst the conversation was taking place. Then, becoming more serious, he surmised, 'It'll take us way too long to go up and start moving along the face from here. We'll have to chance doing it from nearer to the house. According to Lacey, the bedrooms are on this side and, seeing there's only the two of them, with any luck they won't be keeping a watch from there.'

Advancing with great caution and constantly scanning the windows of the building for any suggestion that they were being observed, the Sheriff and the patrolman were about forty yards closer before they again came to a halt. This was not caused by the discovery, or possibility, that they had been detected. Instead, at that point, they noticed a rift in the face which appeared to go right to the top of the cliff. As there was otherwise a slightly overhanging ridge along the top, they concluded they had found the one spot at which they might most easily be able to reach the summit. It would, they also realized, be considerably more easy and safe to walk the remaining distance along the top than at ground level, or by sidling to their destination across the face of the cliff.

On being reached, not without the expenditure of considerable exertion to attain the position as quickly yet silently as possibly, the peace officers found the rift was no more than four feet wide and about thirty-four inches deep. Nevertheless, it presented complete shelter and protection from being seen by the occupants of the building. As the area was beyond the glare thrown by the spotlights, it also reduced the chance of anybody on Route 228 noticing them.

Unfortunately, the satisfactory state of affairs did not last!

'God damn it, Joe!' Jack growled, halting after having

crawled upwards for some fifteen feet, with his companion following him. 'I thought things were going just a mite too god-damned easily. You can't see it from below, but the son-of-a-bitch peters out just before we pass that dad-blasted overhang.'

'There's some who reckon life's no fun without a challenge,' Garrity gritted, having been just as convinced as the Sheriff that they could reach the top by the present means. 'But *I'm* not one of them!'

'Or me!' Jack seconded.

At that moment, one of the fugitives started yelling!

On this occasion, Jack and Garrity had no difficulty in hearing the message!

'It's been over half an hour, you ''mother-something'' Fascist pigs! You've got just five more minutes before we waste one of these god-damned *Chicano* tail-peddlers and toss her down there to prove we're not bluffing!'

Although neither of the radicals realized it, the derogatory way in which the speaker referred to the hostages had been a serious error in tactics!

* * *

Having finally been allowed to pass through the road block maintaining 'Operation Gob-Stopper', the reporter from the *Gusher City Mirror* and the female television newscaster were delayed even further before reaching their destination. Acting upon the instructions of the Senior Deputy Sheriff, a couple of Highway Patrol officers on motor cycles — who had been on the way to offer assistance at the incident — had stopped them when they exceeded the speed limit of fifty-five miles per hour in an attempt to make up for the lost time. Having the kind of nature which resented having its wishes thwarted in the slightest degree, neither was feeling at his or her most amiable when they arrived. However, being of a cautious mould, the newspaperman delayed leaving his car so as

46

to allow the woman to take the lead in lodging the complaints.

Watching the tall, almost painfully slim, newscaster leap from the front seat of the small truck with her fairly good looking face and demeanour redolent of self-righteous indignation, Captain Bellamy remembered something Brenda Tragg had said about her after watching one of her virulent tirades against the local law enforcement agencies. 'Except that she's nowhere nearly so superlatively brilliant and intelligent as *they* are always shown to be, she might be a clone of those middle class "liberal", "Women's Lib" stereotypes who play the noble Public Defender in practically every television "cop" show.' He considered the description to be apt. Dressed in a severely masculine fashion, as was mandatory except for the inevitable scene when bedded down with a 'hero' of similar political persuasions, her brunette hair was long and straight.

'All right!' Faith Robertus snarled, stalking forward and thrusting her face very close to that of the Watch Commander. 'What the "something" hell is coming off?'

'Coming off, ma'am?' Bellamy asked blandly, controlling his natural revulsion at hearing profanity from a person whose educational standards ought to have rendered the need for it unnecessary.

'You know what I mean!' the newscaster stated, with truth as she suspected. 'Why the "something" were we stopped getting here?'

'*Stopped*, ma'am?' Bellamy queried. 'Seems to me like you're *here*.'

'*Delayed*, then!' Faith corrected, her voice rising and its Mid-West accent becoming more pronounced.

'Just you?' Bellamy asked, seeming to grow calmer as the wrath of the newscaster increased.

'Y — Well no,' Faith admitted, making the revision with obvious reluctance. 'The deputies *were* stopping everybody, but they wouldn't let me go through.'

'You mean they wouldn't let you go through ahead of

47

the folks who were there already and waiting?'

'I showed them my press card —!' the newscaster asserted, in a manner suggesting such a document invested superior rights and privileges upon the bearer.

'And I reckon they'd've been right pleased to honour it, ma'am,' the Watch Commander interrupted, with such sincerity he might have been speaking the truth on oath. 'Trouble being, those good tax paying folks ahead of you mightn't've taken kindly to you being passed through before them. It could even have struck them as *favouritism*.'

'That's not all!' Faith claimed, her sallow cheeks reddening, but the suggestion of her being suspected of receiving favours from the hated "pigs" was sufficient to prevent her continuing her first line of complaint. 'Those "mother-some —" — They made me and my men each read and tell them we *understood* what was meant by the "disclaimer" they insisted we all sign before they would let us pass.'

'That's standard procedure, as laid down by the County Commissioners, ma'am,' Bellamy replied and, despite his best efforts, he could not restrain just a trace of satisfaction from coming into his otherwise impersonal tone. 'We have to be *real* sure folks know what's coming down and don't lay the blame on us should they or their vehicle get shot up as they pass. It's bad public relations for us otherwise, if they should be.'

'What's happening here?' the newscaster asked, so hurriedly it was obvious she had no desire to go further into the matter under discussion.

There was a good reason for the reticence being shown by the young woman. She was to blame for that aspect of the delay.

Some time earlier, after a man had had his car riddled by bullets — fortunately, none of which hit him — while passing a point where police were attempting to dislodge the two criminals shooting from a warehouse, Faith had persuaded him to sue the G.C.P.D. Although he had lost the case when he had admitted ignoring warnings of the danger, the Department of Public Safety had taken precautions against a repetition. At the instigation of Jack Tragg, whenever similar situations arose, people approaching the area were informed of the situation and, if they decided to go on, were required to sign a 'disclaimer' statement absolving the authorities of all responsibility for any injury or damage which might occur.

Not only had the newscaster failed in her attempt to humiliate and discredit the municipal law enforcement agency, she had inadvertently paved the way for her delayed arrival at the scene of the present incident and in the circumstances she could hardly complain.

'One of our House's black and whites chased a couple of "suspects" from the scene of a double killing —,' Bellamy began.

'Had they done the killings?' Faith challenged.

'Well now, I can't give a definite affirmatory to that,' the Watch Commander confessed, in a judicial fashion which only just avoided blatant sarcasm. 'But the Morenos were killed with a heavy calibre automatic pistol and an Armalite carbine, both of which the "suspects" are armed with. We won't know for sure whether it was them or not until F.I.L.[1] have run a comparison check on bullets from their weapons and those used to kill the Morenos.'

'*Morenos*?'

'They were the victims and as nice a middle-aged couple of Hispanics as I've had the pleasure of knowing.'

'*Hispanics*?' the newscaster repeated and her voice had lost some of its suggestion of sympathy for the 'suspects'.

'Sure,' Bellamy confirmed, satisfied that the conversation was going the way he wanted. 'And there's no way they could have done anything to *justify* the "suspects"

---

1. '*F.I.L.*': the Firearms Investigation Laboratory of the Scientific Investigation Bureau, based in the Department of Public Safety Building and manned by technicians of the Gusher City Police Department. J.T.E.

shooting them. I've *tried* to get Papa Moreno to keep a gun on hand, but he wouldn't.'

'Those god-damned yoyos *claim* they're a couple of radical "freedom fighters" and are asking to be flown out of the country to somewhere they'll be safe from the F.B.I.,' Oliver Lacey announced, walking forward from where he had been listening to what was said. Ignoring the furious glare directed his way by Bellamy, he went on, 'There's one thing I can't figure out, though. If they *are* what they claim, why would they ask to be flown to San Salvador?'

'*San Salvador*?' Faith asked. 'But that's in —!'

'El Salvador,' said the businessman, completing the unfinished sentence. 'I know they said Cuba when they called the *Mirror* and your studio, but as soon as they hung up one of them told the other to yell down and ask for a flight to San Salvador.'

'But why would they want to go *there*?' the newscaster demanded, being aware that — although left wing 'freedom fighters' were operating a terrorist campaign there — the Government of El Salvador would not offer sanctuary to the 'suspects' if they were of such political persuasions.

'I got the notion they were just putting your people and the *Mirror* on about being radicals,' Lacey explained, his features so innocent of guile it would have taken a completely sceptical person to mistrust him. 'After they'd called, one of them told me they were sure to get the support of you cruddie Commies in the media by making out they were the same kind of Pinko crap.'

Listening to the conversation, Bellamy needed all his considerable ability as a poker player to retain an impassive demeanour. He silently conceded he had been doing the plump businessman an injustice. By playing upon the 'liberal' proclivity towards ethnic buttlicking, whereby no member of a minority group could *ever* be in the wrong, he had reduced the eagerness of the newscaster and the reporter from the Mirror — who had come over without

50

joining the discussion — to lend moral support to the 'suspects'. At first, he had mentally cursed Lacey for doing what he was hoping to avoid by allowing them to learn the nature of the men against whom his party was in contention. Now he realized he was wrong. Far from ruining his efforts, Lacey had given him immeasurable support. Neither representative of the media believed radicals wishing to flee the United States would want to be taken to the capital city of a country ruled by a very firm Right Wing Government.

'The other one said he wondered if they'd get to use naptham to zap the Commies there like they had in 'Nam,' the businessman continued, having recognized the new-comers and guessed what lay behind their delayed appearance on the scene, he had thought up a means by which he could help the peace officers. 'Which made me think maybe they weren't figuring on *joining* the "freedom —"!'

At that moment, the man in the house made a statement which — apart from the reference to 'Fascist pigs' — seemed to give credence to the story Lacey was telling.

'The sheriff's on his way now!' Sergeant Bulpin announced over the megaphone, with complete veracity; although not in the context which it was hoped the two radicals would accept the declaration. 'He'll be here soon!'

* * *

'Fun's over, Joe!' Jack Tragg said quietly over his shoulder. 'Ready or not, we've got to call it a "go".'

'This is *fun*?' Patrolman Garrity replied.

Continuing to wriggle up the narrow rift until he estimated they were as far as it was possible to go above the roof, the Sheriff edged slowly out of its protection. Followed by his companion, he clung precariously to the side of the cliff. At that moment, neither of them underestimated the danger. Rapid movement was impossible. If they should be spotted by the radicals, the range was so short even the one armed with the Colt Government Model automatic pistol would be unlikely to miss.

Yet, desperate though the position of the two peace officers undoubtedly would be in such circumstances, it was not completely untenable!

Neither was it a sinecure!

While Jack and Garrity were now fully exposed to view, the beams of the spotlights coming from Route 228 were glaring against the cliff above and below them. On a darker night, the contrast might have rendered them close to invisible. However, under the prevailing conditions — in spite of realizing it was unlikely to be the case — the bright moonlight had the effect of making each of them feel as if he was facing an audience on a well lit stage.

Slowly and with extreme care, the peace officers continued to move in the direction of their objective. There was now, each appreciated, an even greater urgency required to ensure every place upon which a foot was rested or a hand grasped could be trusted to hold. Not only was there an increased danger of slipping but a piece of loosened rock falling to the ground would almost certainly be heard inside the house and bring at least one of the radicals to investigate.

At last, Jack felt that safety was practically attained!

The Sheriff was within fifteen feet of the building and some twenty feet higher than the nearest window. Even if one of the fugitives happened to look out, he could not see the approaching peace officers unless he should turn his gaze upwards for some reason. There did not appear to be any cause for him to do so.

Letting out a sigh of relief as he was groping for another hand hold, Jack chanced to glance downwards!

What the Sheriff saw caused him to freeze with his arm extended and crooked fingers just clear of the crack for which he had been reaching!

A figure was standing at the nearest window, which was slightly ajar!

The face was *upturned*!

The eyes were staring straight at the peace officers!

4   It's the Sheriff

For a single, breath-taking and heart-stopping instant, which seemed to be a vastly longer period of time, Jack Tragg thought it was one of the radicals gazing at him!

Then the Sheriff realized he was being studied by a pretty, curvaceous and stylishly dressed girl of obvious Hispanic birthright!

In spite of having established the gender of the observer, however, Jack was painfully aware that his position might not be any more of a sinecure than if either Richard Cleverly or Edward Gierek were looking at him. He had been detected by a person who, although the law enforcement agencies of Rockabye County were far from oppressive where prostitutes were concerned as long as they were well behaved, might have a real or imagined grudge against peace officers in general. Or she could believe the pretence of the fugitives that they were stalwart protectors of the 'poor and downtrodden' ethnic minorities, so might feel it incumbent upon herself to alert them to the danger she had discovered.

In either case, the life expectancies of the Sheriff of Rockabye County and Patrolman Joseph Garrity would be far from extensive!

Nor, Jack suspected, would the black harness bull qualifying as a member of a leading 'poor and downtrodden' ethnic minority group prevent either of the radicals from opening fire upon him!

Even as the Sheriff was drawing his unpalatable conclusions, but before he could even start to decide upon a line

54

of defensive action, the girl looked over her shoulder!

To add to his consternation, Jack saw another figure was approaching the window with rapid strides!

The newcomer was male and the colour of his hair identified him as Edward Gierek!

If either of the peace officers had been able to draw a weapon and take the simplest way out of their difficulties, the brown haired radical would have presented them with an easy target as he was crossing the room. Although he was pulling the Colt Government Model automatic pistol from his belt, as yet he was displaying no sign of being aware of their presence.

Unfortunately, even if their training and ethics would have permitted such an action without direct provocation, the Sheriff and the patrolman each required both his hands to continue clinging to the face of the cliff!

In fact, Jack had been compelled to complete the movement he was making when becoming aware that he was being watched!

Should either the Sheriff or Garrity so much as attempt to reach for his holstered revolver, he would immediately be precipitated backwards to the ground!

Gierek spoke!

However, the words were not directed at the all but helpless peace officers!

'Just what the "mother-something" hell are you up to?' the radical demanded, sharing with Faith Robertus and numerous other middle class 'liberals' an outlook which considered that the frequent use of profanity in mixed company expressed a willingness to come down to the level of the 'little people.'

'Just what I told you I would be,' the girl replied, in accent free English. Her tone implied resentment and hostility as she elaborated, 'I've been to the john. Where else?'

Having been on the point of telling the patrolman to take a chance and jump, the Sheriff refrained!

Clearly, regardless of her illegal way of earning a living,

the prostitute did not intend to denounce the peace officers!

'Are you sure you weren't planning to split?' Gierek challenged, glancing at rather than through the partially open window.

'You don't think I'd leave Cousin Rosa alone with you two, do you?' the girl replied with cold dignity, then continued after hesitating for a moment, clearly to think up an acceptable excuse for her behaviour, 'Seeing as your *friends* from the media haven't come rushing out to help you, I thought I'd find out what the fuzz are doing.'

'What are they doing?' the radical demanded, stepping forward.

'A Buick sedan drove up just now,' Maria Esteban lied, pointing towards the road. 'It's the Sheriff come at last.'

For all the words and courageous behaviour of the girl, Jack knew the danger to the patrolman and himself was not at an end!

If Gierek happened to glance upwards instead of in the direction being indicated by the prostitute, all would be lost!

And not only for the peace officers!

The radical would almost certainly kill the girl for what he would consider to be an act of betrayal!

The problem did not arise!

Although Gierek pushed Maria aside and went to stand at the window, his gaze turned immediately towards the area at which she had pointed!

'Where the "something" hell is that "mother-something" Buick?' the radical demanded looking over his shoulder towards the girl after having stared out of the window for what seemed to the prostitute, and the two peace officers clinging precariously to the face of the cliff, to have been a considerably longer time than was actually the case. 'I can't see anything of it on the road, or the "mother-something" Sheriff either.'

'It kept going,' Maria answered, striving to prevent the growing tension she was feeling from becoming apparent

56

in her voice and demeanour. 'You don't think he'd be *loco* enough to stop his heap and get out where that *amigo* of yours could have a clear blast at him. Sheriffs are only that stupid in *The Dukes Of Hazzard*, or *B.J. And The Bear*.'

'Is that so, you greaser whore?' Gierek asked, employing a term which no Hollywood "liberal" script writer would have thought to put into the mouth of a noble radical activist in conflict against the evil Capitalist Establishment. He was annoyed at the disdain shown to two television series he regarded highly for their anti-law and order content. 'And maybe it wasn't his heap you saw?'

'It was him all right, you can bet on that,' Maria asserted, stiffened in her resolve by the racist slur. 'You think I don't know super-heat's heap when I see it, maybe?'

Without waiting for a response from the clearly annoyed radical, the prostitute turned and walked defiantly across the room. Watching her move, the sheriff was filled with admiration for her courage and strength of will. He had detected a mounting timbre of worry in her tone and perturbation in her manner. For all that, there was nothing in her bearing as she was taking her departure to suggest she was even slightly aware of the terrible gamble she was making.

After Maria had disappeared from the view of the men outside the building, Gierek let out an angry snort and returned his gaze to the window. Only briefly, however. Nor did he look upwards. Conducting his scrutiny of the road for a few seconds, he once more snorted and shrugged his shoulders. Then, returning the automatic pistol to his belt, he swung around to follow her.

'Whooee!' Garrity breathed, remembering the girl as one who used Gusher City South Division as a base for her illegal transactions. 'I owe you one, Maria!'

'We both do!' seconded Jack, just as quietly and with equal vehemence.

Neither peace officer gave the matter any thought, but

the behaviour of the prostitute was a tribute to the fair dealing and general standard of conduct insisted upon by the Sheriff and Chief of Police Phineas Hagen.

With their respective sentiments uttered, Jack and the patrolman resumed their interrupted advance!

As he was once more moving along the face, the Sheriff found he was now deliberately keeping his gaze straight ahead and avoiding so much as glancing at the windows of the building. He realized that, as a defensive measure, this was no more effective than the proverbial ostrich burying its head in the sand. For all that, he could not restrain himself from behaving in such a fashion. Being so close to his goal, he told himself grimly if silently, he had no intention of stopping again. Not even if one of the radicals was to lean out of a window and yell, or opened fire, at him. One way or another, his sole desire at that moment was to have the ordeal over.

What was more, when discussing the incident afterwards, Jack discovered Garrity had been subject to similar emotions and had behaved in an identical fashion.

Suddenly and shockingly, the Sheriff realized he was caught in the full glare of a spotlight!

Even as he was being assailed by a sensation of furious outrage, brought about through the assumption that somebody on Route 228 had been so careless as to direct the brilliant beam upon him, Jack glanced downwards. He received a most welcome surprise. No such error had been committed. Instead, he had finally arrived in the illuminated area. This meant, being at last directly over the roof of the building, he was now safe from the view of any of the occupants. Furthermore, unless something untoward happened, it would only be a matter of seconds before Garrity too was in a similarly safe position.

Working his way downwards, employing just as much caution as he had while making the crossing, regardless of his feeling of relief, the Sheriff contrived to step over and arrive upon the flat roof. A glance around told him that the patrolman was behaving with an equal care. Then, a few seconds later, having been just as successful in making the transfer without noise, his companion joined him.

'Should I *ever* be *loco* enough to volunteer for a caper like *this* again, sir,' the burly black harness bull requested, in a whisper charged with relief. 'Take pity on my poor old mammy's half-witted lil boy — and say, "No way"!'

'I'll keep it in mind,' Jack promised, wiping perspiration from his brow.

'All right already, you "mother-something" Fascist pigs!' Richard Cleverly yelled, from somewhere ahead and below the peace officers. 'We know the "mother-something" sheriff's arrived and we're out of patience. How about it?'

'You heard Dick!' Gierek supplemented when, in accordance with the instructions he had received from Jack, Sergeant David Bulpin had not replied after a few seconds. 'We're pee'd off with waiting and are coming down. Either you let us through, you "mother-something" sons-of-bitches, or you're going to have a couple of very dead *Chicano* hookers on your hands to explain away.'

Walking across the roof on tiptoe, grateful to discover it was justifying the confidence expressed by Oliver Lacey in its sturdy construction (he had claimed it would support the weight of the two peace officers without giving any indication of their presence). Jack halted just clear of the front edge. Although concealed from anybody inside the building, he was exposed to the law enforcement officers and other spectators on the road. Not that he remained in their sight for long. Giving a wave and having it returned immediately by Bulpin, he turned and followed Garrity who — having kept out of view — was already stepping quietly towards the eastern end.

The appearance of the Sheriff had been of such brief duration, neither the reporter from the *Gusher City Mirror* nor the television newscaster and her crew had noticed him. Having accepted the story regarding the political affiliations of the fugitives told by Lacey, none of them were paying any particular attention to the way in which the operation was being conducted. Although she would have suggested an acceptance of their terms if she had known the truth about the radicals, Faith Robertus had not raised any objections on being informed that it was unlikely these would be met and she was willing to wait until Jack Tragg put in an appearance in the hope of making some kind of capital from what she otherwise considered to be a waste of her time.

'This is Captain Bellamy of the G.C.P.D.!' the Watch Commander from the Gusher City South Division announced, having gone over to take the megaphone from Bulpin. 'It must have been me you saw come, the Sheriff isn't down here yet. But we've had word from him and he says we've got to be shown proof that both girls are still alive and unharmed before we can consider agreeing to your terms.'

'They're alive!' Gierek stated.

'And unharmed!' Bellamy countered.

'They're *unarmed*!' the brunette radical asserted indignantly. 'God damn it, even if Dick and I weren't into Gay-Lib, do you think we'd be wasting our time raping a couple of god-damned greaser hookers?'

'Let the girls show themselves on the porch where we can see them!' the Watch Commander demanded. 'The aircraft's ready and waiting, but you're not coming through until I'm satisfied they're both all right.'

'We'll have to go along with him, Ed!' Cleverly advised. 'Send them out, I can drop them both if they try to run away.'

'If you have to,' Gierek pointed out, 'that won't help us!'

'It will help *them* a lot less,' the blond answered. 'Anyway, you don't think a couple of god-damned hookers will let themselves get wasted to help the pigs, do you?' Making a derisive gesture with the Armalite carbine in the direction of the two girls, he went on in a mocking tone, 'How about it, do either of you feel like sacrificing yourselves?'

'Like hell we do!' Maria declared vehemently. While the radicals were talking to the peace officers she had taken the opportunity to inform her cousin of the discovery she had made in the bedroom. Knowing herself to be the stronger personality, she had already ordered Rosa Moreno to let her do all the talking and she continued, 'But there's something you two had better remember, particularly you, *hombre bravo* with the carbine. There's no way the fuzz are going to let you get a car to the airport unless they're certain we're in it, alive and kicking.'

'Don't let *that* worry you,' Gierek growled. 'Having you pair along is our ticket to Cuba. So you can show yourselves and let them know I meant what I said about wasting you if there are any tricks.'

'And keep *this* in mind all the time you're out there,' Cleverly went on, smarting under the contemptuous way he had been addressed as, "*hombre bravo*", "brave man", as he once again waved his weapon. 'You just look like you're trying to leave the porch and you'll be too dead to care what happens to us.'

'*Senores el policia!*' Maria shouted, as she and her cousin stepped on to the porch covered by the carbine and automatic pistol in the hands of the fugitives. Having sufficient faith in the local law enforcement agencies to feel sure they would do everything possible to avoid injury to herself and Rosa, she hoped to learn whether they wanted any kind of action taken and went on speaking in Spanish. '*Que paso, por favor* —!'

'Speak English, you "mother-something" greaser whore or I'll give you something worse than your social disease!' Cleverly yelled, inadvertantly helping the men on the roof by prolonging the conversation and further delaying the departure of his party. 'Don't try to get smart-assed with us!'

'And stop right where you are!' Gierek supplemented.

'Whatever you say, *comrade*,' Maria answered, too quietly for the words to be heard on Route 228. She was wondering whether she and her cousin were supposed to

61

make a dash from the porch and allow the peace officers, whom she deduced were on the roof, to drop between themselves and the radicals. Concluding that to make such an attempt would be dangerous in the extreme, after a moment's thought, she felt sure it was not contemplated. Deciding against making the attempt, or trying the patience of the already excitably nervous pair too far, she raised her voice again and went on in English, 'Hey, Captain Bellamy, can you hear me?'

'What did you say?' the Watch Commander inquired, unable to see if the sheriff and patrolmen were ready, so playing for time in case it should be needed by them. 'You'll have to speak louder!'

'I said —!' Maria began, fighting against the temptation to look upwards as doing so might alert the radicals to the help she believed was on the roof.

'Speak louder and move forward to give us a better chance of hearing you!' Bellamy suggested, without any great hope that his instructions would be permitted.

The assumption proved correct!

'Get the hell back in here!' Gierek ordered savagely and, while the girls were obeying as slowly as Maria estimated would be safe, he shouted without leaving the building or appearing in the doorway, 'That's it with the talking, you "mother-something" Fascist pigs. You've seen they're both alive and unharmed. So now, whether you're ready or not, we're bringing them down and it's up to *you* whether they live or die.'

'We know the media's down there with you by this time!' the blond radical went on, being disinclined to let it appear his companion was conducting the negotiations in the capacity of leader. Unaware of the trick which had been played by Lacey to deprive them of the publicity they desired, he elaborated with a complete lack of diplomacy. 'So just remember, while they might only be a couple of no-account hookers to you, they're both Hispanics and their people won't sit back quietly if they get wasted because you "mother-something" Fascist pigs didn't care enough about them to let us come through and fly out.'

'Don't loose your cool!' Bellamy countered, glancing at the television newscaster and the reporter, wondering whether they now suspected the businessman had lied when describing the political persuasions of the fugitives who had invaded his home. There was nothing in the attitude of either to suggest this was the case. In fact, he concluded the ill-advised manner in which the last comment in particular had been phrased had struck each as being further evidence to support the claims made by Lacey and neither was willing to show the sympathy which they would have displayed if they had known they were listening to left wing extremists. Satisfied that "Operation Gob-Stopper" was still effective, due to the unasked — but nevertheless most welcome — support of the businessman, he continued, 'We're satisfied that they're all right. You can drive on down with them as soon as you're ready and we'll let you come through.'

5 One advantage of being black

'Know something, sir?' Patrolman Joseph Garrity commented dryly, listening to the way in which Richard Cleverly was ordering Maria Esteban to speak English as he and the Sheriff of Rockabye County were coming to a halt at the eastern edge of the roof. 'I've *never* heard a radical activist in a television "cop" show call a hooker a name like that and her a *Chicano* to boot.'

'Or me,' Jack Tragg admitted, just as sardonically. 'In fact, ever since Hanoi Jane made *Klute*, the Hollywood "liberals" have treated prostitution as if it was a honourable and desirable profession and that kind of talk is always reserved for us evil Southron W.A.S.P. racists in their scripts. I tell you, Joe, if those two good old boys don't watch what they're saying, their buddies from the media down there might get taken with the notion they're not radical activists at all.'

'Was I one for billing into other people's doings, I'd warn them about it,' the big black patrolman declared, starting to uncoil the short length of rope which encircled his waist. Nodding over his shoulder while doing so, he continued, 'Good for Maria, though, she's still playing the game for us. I only wish there was some way we could have told her what we're figuring on doing, so she and the other girl don't make any wrong moves.'

'So do I,' the Sheriff confessed, also glancing to where the prostitute was still doing her best to keep the conversation going. 'But something tells me she could have figured it out for herself.'

'There's one way *you* could have made certain sure she'd know, sir,' Garrity stated, looping and drawing tight the ready made noose at one end of the rope around the metal air vent which protruded from the roof.

'How?' Jack inquired.

'I've heard tell you can speak Spanish so good you can pass as a *Chicano*,' the patrolman explained with a broad grin, allowing the free end of the rope to fall over the edge of the roof. 'Which being, you could have started *singing* what we're figuring on doing in Mex' and she'd have understood, but neither of those yoyos would because they don't *habla Espanol*.'

'I did so think about trying just that,' the Sheriff protested, aware of his linguistic ability being common knowledge among the members of the county and municipal law enforcement agencies. He was, in fact, one of the few Caucasian peace officers in Rockabye County who the legal profession — albeit reluctantly in some cases, no pun intended — considered sufficiently fluent to be competent to "read his rights" in Spanish to a person of Hispanic "roots".[1] 'Trouble being, I didn't think either of our hairy "comrades" down there would be *quite* stupid enough to mistake us for a couple of good old *Chicano* boys out a-serenading their *amantes* in the moonlight; especially from on the roof. So we'll just have to count on Maria having the smarts to make the right guess and finding a chance to put the other girl wise.'

Having concluded the comment, part of a conversation carried out *sotto voce* for the purpose of helping to reduce the tension which — despite their respective experience in situations involving considerable stress — both were feeling, Jack grasped the rope in both hands and stood astride it facing away from the edge of the roof. The warning given by Cleverly indicated there must be no further delay.

1. *How the 'rights' are 'read' to a suspect in Rockabye County is described in:* APPENDIX FOUR. *An example of how Sheriff Jack Tragg put to use his ability to speak Spanish with great fluency is given in:* THE SHERIFF OF ROCKABYE COUNTY. *J.T.E.*

Tugging on the rope, to ensure the vent was as firm and strong as Oliver Lacey had asserted, he began to slide to the ground. Glancing into one of the windows as he passed, he ascertained that the garage portion of the building was in darkness and unoccupied.

While the height of the wall down which the descent was being made was not so great it would have been unsafe to drop without the assistance of the rope, the sheriff had felt disinclined to take the chance of being heard on landing in such a fashion. The means he had elected to employ made it possible for himself and the patrolman — who followed as soon as he had alighted and stepped clear — to reach the ground in almost complete silence.

Walking quickly to the front entrance of the garage, after having peered around the end of the building to satisfy themselves they could do so without attracting the attention of the radicals, neither Jack nor Garrity were in the least put out by finding it was closed. They had been warned by the owner of the property that such would be the case and he had also supplied the means with which they could gain admittance.

The main door was one of the wide, 'roll up' variety which could be operated via an electronic device while approaching in a vehicle. Although Lacey had left behind the control box, this presented no obstacle for the peace officers. They would not have used it even if it had been available to them, as they had known the sound of the mechanism being put into motion would have warned the radicals of their presence. There was another and, for their purposes, far safer means of effecting an entrance. Fortunately, the businessman had not been searched before he was sent to deliver the ultimatum from Cleverly and Edward Gierek. One of the keys on the ring in his trousers pocket was for the lock of the smaller, pedestrian's door alongside the main entrance.

Making use of the key he had had given to him by Lacey, Jack unlocked and opened the door, moving with considerable caution, in case the departure of the radicals and their hostages had already commenced. Hearing nothing to suggest this was the case and looking inside with an equal care, he concluded everything was pretty close to being as he required. The interior lights were out and the angle from Route 228 was sufficient to ensure no beam from the spotlights below could probe directly through the windows on the side. In spite of that, even when the door was closed, there still would be sufficient reflected glow from outside to offer all the necessary illumination for what he and the patrolman had come to do.

Passing the Sheriff, carrying his Colt Python .357 Magnum revolver drawn ready for use, Garrity swung a sweeping gaze around. There were two cars in the garage, a Cadillac sedan belonging to Lacey and the Ford Mustang in which the two prostitutes had arrived for their uncompleted assignation. Even with the vehicles inside, there was still a reasonable amount of empty space.

'Whooee!' the burly patrolman breathed, as his companion entered and, by closing the door, brought an end to the direct illumination from the road. 'I wish *my* garage was even close to this tidy.'

'Your wife rides you about it too, huh?' Jack inquired sympathetically and just as quietly. Receiving an affirmatory nod, he continued, 'I always thought, seeing how nature isn't supposed to make the same mistake *twice*, no two women could be alike. See happen you can fix the main light while I attend to the connecting door.'

'Yo!' assented the patrolman, wondering if there would be time for the precautions to be taken before the radicals arrived.

Going to the Cadillac without commenting upon the point, Garrity holstered his revolver and climbed on to its hood. Aided by the extra height he acquired by doing so, he reached upwards and twisted the long, tubular fluorescent lamp free from its 'bayonet mount' fitting in the roof. Lifting it clear, he lowered it and himself carefully to the floor. Then, remembering the favourable remarks made by the Sheriff about the owner of the vehicle while they were taking a breather during the climb, he leaned the tube against its side and used the right sleeve of his dark blue uniform shirt to remove the few marks his feet had made on the hood.

While the patrolman was elminating one potential source of illumination which might otherwise have placed the rescue attempt at jeopardy, Jack was taking a similar precaution. However, his task was somewhat easier to accomplish. Crossing to the door which gave access to the living quarters of the building and which was bathed in shadows, he placed his ear against it to listen for a moment. Hearing nothing to suggest there could be need for haste, or to warn his companion, he unscrewed the electric light bulb from its socket above the door and placed it upon one of the uncluttered shelves the sight of which, in part, had provoked the envious comment from Garrity as they had entered the garage. Having done this, he once more listened for any information to indicate what was happening beyond the dividing wall.

'I can't hear anything from them yet,' the Sheriff remarked, as his companion joined him. 'So now all we have to do is wait.'

'Like they always used to tell us at the Academy,' the patrolman replied. 'Waiting's often what police work is all about.'

'Well now,' Jack drawled with a grin, despite having the greatest respect for the high standard of training instilled by the Academy of the Gusher City Police Department. 'I'm real pleased to hear they teach you something *right* there.'

'Why they surely so do,' Garrity agreed, knowing there was no malice in the apparently derogatory remark and also grinning. 'They teach us *always* to call every newly-made deputy sheriff "*sir*" all polite and respectful, even though he isn't in *the* Department.' Then the levity departed and he put aside all thought of the friendly rivalry which existed between the municipal police officers and members of the Sheriff's Office, going on soberly,

'Mind if I make a suggestion, sir?'

'Feel free,' Jack authorized, pausing although he had been on the point of taking up his position for the ambush which the delay in the arrival of the radicals and hostages was making possible.

'Maybe it would be better happen *I* was to stand *that* side of the door, sir,' the patrolman offered, nodding in the direction selected by the Sheriff. 'One advantage of being black is I don't show up so well in the shadows as a honky like you.'

'Have it *your* way, *amigo*,' Jack accepted, after a moment's hesitation which was *not* in any way caused by resentment over how the suggestion was worded. He had selected his intended position instinctively and without even thinking of his companion being black. Crossing to stand just beyond the hinged side of the door, he glanced and went on, 'By cracky, Joe, you're right at that. You don't show up at all,'

Despite being aware that they were waiting to waylay a pair of fugitives, who would not hestitate an instant before trying to kill them if offered an opportunity, neither of the peace officers followed the hoary fictional cliche of taking out his revolver and checking upon the contents of its cylinder.[2] Nor, although each was aware he might need to arm himself with great rapidity — despite intending to tackle and capture the radicals with bare hands if possible — did either offer to ensure his weapon 'hung loosely in its holster'. A rig which necessitated such a precaution before use would be more of a liability than an aid to survival. Being cognizant of that basic gun fighting fact, the Rockabye County Department of Public Safety laid down such a high standard of acceptance in 'Threads and Pieces' — the name given by the local peace officers

2. *Even the late and* very *great John Wayne can be seen performing such a check of his revolver in his 1975 movie,* BRANNIGAN. *However, in exculpation, we believe the 'Duke' only did this to establish for late comers in the cinema audience that — despite the action taking place in 'gun free' London, England — he was armed. J.T.E.*

to its *Manual Of Dress And Armaments' Regulations* — that the rules precluded any chance of so ill advised a selection being made when purchasing this most vitally important piece of equipment.

Once the ambush positions had been attained, a contingency which Jack had taken into account when making plans on Route 228, hoping that the chance to put this aspect into effect would be presented as it would offer himself and Garrity an element of surprise, time began to drag by with what seemed an interminable slowness.

However, in the course of their respective service as peace officers, the Sheriff and the patrolman had each performed sufficient stake-out duties to have learned the value of patience. Neither spoke, cleared his throat, shuffled his feet, nor moved any more than was absolutely necessary. Even when some slight motion could not be avoided, care was taken to hold its noise to a minimum.

At first, in fact, Jack and Garrity were far from displeased by the respite. It was offering them an opportunity to throw off the last effects of the not inconsiderable exertions which had been required to ascend the slope, move along the face of the cliff and reach the interior of the garage.

Gradually, however, a disturbing thought began to occur to each peace officer!

A more than sufficient time had elapsed since their arrival for the party from the living quarters to have put in an appearance!

Yet there still was not the slightest indication that the intended departure was about to take place!

The same disturbing question sprang almost simultaneously to the minds of the waiting lawmen!

Had the radicals suspected a trap had been laid and changed their minds about leaving?

If that should be the case, Jack and Garrity realized, the danger to the two prostitutes would be increased immeasurably!

At least one of the girls would almost certainly be killed

immediately, so as to offer convincing proof of the determination to obtain an unimpeded escape not only from the building but out of the country which was motivating the fugitives. Or, should they have decided their demands would not be met regardless of what they had been told by Captain Henry Bellamy, the 'harmless' *marijuana* — augmented by whatever form of 'hard' narcotic they were using to boost their courage — might lead the pair to murder both their captives and try to flee overland on foot in search of other hostages.

No matter which happened, or even if something equally adverse that neither peace officer had conceived should occur, the situation which they had taken so many risks and expended so much energy to avert was likely to be brought to fruition!

Appreciating the ramifications if any adverse eventuality take place, Garrity felt sympathy for his companion!

The patrolman knew that if the affair should turn out badly, even though the failure was through no fault of his and due to circumstances which could not be foreseen, the sheriff would be held responsible!

At that moment, the black peace officer was grateful for his decision to remain a uniformed harness bull instead of accepting promotion to the Bureau of Detectives. While the old saying that 'rank has its privileges' was undoubtedly true, acquiring it also brought an ever growing volume of responsibility in its wake. He now realized more than ever that under many circumstances, as senior member of the law enforcement agencies on the scene of an incident, it required a special kind of man to make the decision upon whatever line of action was to be taken and know that the life of another human being hung in the balance.

Jack Tragg was such a man!

Watching and waiting in the semi darkness, Garrity hoped all would go well and the moral courage displayed by the Sheriff of Rockabye County in selecting how they should conduct themselves would receive the reward it deserved!

Suddenly, after what seemed to the waiting peace officers to have been hours — but in reality was no more than fifteen minutes — the brass knob of the door at which each had been staring began to move!

There had been no sound from beyond the dividing wall to announce such an action was due to take place!

6 Another advantage of being black

'God damn it!' snarled the voice of Edward Garrity, the words grating and whining as if being ejected by nerves strung tightly and almost to breaking point. To the accompaniment of a switch being operated several times in rapid succession, he went on, 'Now the son-of-a-bitching lights in the garage aren't working!'

Listening to the complaint and watching the connecting door which gave access to the living quarters starting to move, Jack Tragg and Patrolman Joseph Garrity knew the passive part of their ordeal had come to an end!

'So why do we need the god-damned lights to get the "mother-something" heap out?' challenged Richard Cleverly, his tone expressing a similar suggestion of tension coming close to hysterical rage. 'Come on, for "something's" sake. We've wasted enough "something" time already, looking for the god-damned keys *you* let him take with him.'

'I can't watch *everything*!' Gierek protested, with something close to childish petulance. 'Besides, who was it thought of using these two's wheels?' When there was no reply from his companion, he went on, 'Get going, you *Chicano* whores!'

In spite of having received an indication that the scheme was at last going as they required and, inadvertently, being offered an explanation for the delay, neither the Sheriff of Rockabye County nor his burly black companion drew his revolver!

Instead, Jack and Garrity tensed ready to go into action

73

as the former had decided they would — should a suitable opportunity be presented — while he was explaining his intentions prior to them setting out from Route 228.

However, there had been one major change in the arrangements!

For once, while working with a subordinate peace officer, the Sheriff was not in the position of greatest danger!

Having accepted the suggestion made by Garrity, Jack was standing at the hinged side of the door. As this opened *into* the garage, it would shield him from being seen by the two radicals as they were entering. Therefore, he would be less at risk than the patrolman. What was more, his view of the pair would be seriously restricted. Despite the latter putting him at something of a disadvantage, having complete faith in his companion, he was neither greatly disturbed nor alarmed by the reduction to his range of vision. It would, he knew, only be temporary.

For all that, being the kind of man he was, the Sheriff could not prevent his conscience from nagging over the remembrance of how he was allowing another peace officer — particularly one of lower rank than his own — to be at greater risk than himself!

There was little time, however, for Jack to continue worrying over the point!

Light from the sitting-room of the living quarters flooded into the garage as the door was thrust open. Fortunately, it did not spread to any dangerous extent. Rather it served to throw the wall against which the patrolman was standing into an even deeper shadow. Furthermore, despite the previous semi-gloom, the sudden increase in the illumination did not affect his vision to any noticeable degree. Hardly daring to breath, in case the sound should be heard and draw attention his way, he crouched like some great predatory beast preparing to pounce, waiting for the most appropriate moment at which to launch his attack. It must, he appreciated, be timed absolutely correct if it was to serve its purpose and prevent either of the hostages from being injured or killed.

Luck appeared to be favouring the peace officers!

Holding hands, the two prostitutes came through the doorway instead of being preceded by one of their captors!

It was obvious, however, that Rosa Moreno was in a far more disturbed mental state than her cousin. She was walking, staring straight to her front, in a zombie-like manner. On the other hand, although Maria Esteban was clearly far from being at ease, she was contriving to behave in passably nonchalant fashion. As was suggested by the stiffness with which she was holding her head, she suspected the peace officers were waiting on either side of the door. Street-wise, she was clearly determined to avoid alerting the radicals to the possibility of an ambush. Without allowing her gaze to stray left or right by even so much as a fraction of an inch, she continued to guide her close to terrified cousin towards the vehicles.

'That's another we owe you, Maria-gal!' Garrity thought, watching the prostitute's behaviour with gratification and satisfaction.

Following a couple of paces behind the hostages, with the Armalite Car 15 S.M.G. 'Commando' carbine dangling by the wrist of its butt from his right hand and the muzzle directed at the floor, nothing in the demeanour of the blond radical suggested he or his companion had given any thought to the possibility of a trap having been laid by the peace officers. Or, if the contingency had occurred to them, they had discounted it. An over inflated sense of their respective — if far from mutual in either's case — intelligence, boosted by the repeated use of *marijuana* cigarettes and a recent 'fix' of cocaine, had prevented them from believing the 'Fascist pigs' might have 'had the smarts' to conceive a way to circumvent their scheme for escaping the consequences of their actions.

Instinct, rather than suspicion, led Cleverly to glance to his left as he was crossing the threshold!

At that moment, the wisdom of the suggestion made by Garrity became obvious!

If the Sheriff had taken up the position occupied by the patrolman as he had originally intended, instead of having agreed to stand at the safer side of the doorway, his lighter skin and khaki attire would almost certainly have betrayed his presence in spite of the surrounding darkness. As it was, with his black skin pigmentation and dark blue uniform, Garrity merged sufficiently into murky gloom to avoid being noticed by the cursory glance from the radical.

Wasting no time in congratulating himself upon his forethought, as Cleverly's gaze was turning forward once more without having detected him, the patrolman decided the period of waiting was over!

'*Now*!' Garrity bellowed thunderously, as much to try and paralyze the blond radical with shock for a vitally important instant as to warn the Sheriff of his intentions, and he reached out with his big hands.

On hearing the shout, having been waiting for something of the sort although he was unable to see what had caused it to be uttered, Jack thrust himself from the wall!

Passing beyond the point at which the opening door had concealed what lay behind it, the sheriff noticed from the corner of his eye that Garrity had grasped and was pulling the radical by the left arm!

A startled exclamation burst from Cleverly, being echoed by the yell of alarm to which Gierek gave voice in the sitting-room!

Thrusting his right foot behind him, Jack kicked the door closed. Then he reached and scooped up one of the prostitutes in each arm. Half carrying and half shoving them, he swept the pair and himself to the right so they would be out of the line of fire if the second radical started shooting. Nor did he take the precaution a moment too soon. Although no explosions from the discharges could be heard, four holes suddenly burst through the connecting door. The .45 calibre bullets expelled by the Colt Government Model of 1911 automatic pistol narrowly missed Maria as they flew across the garage to be halted by striking the side of the Ford Mustang.

'God damn it!' the Sheriff thought furiously, the realization striking him of what was portended by the earlier and present absence of noise from the living quarters. 'The son-of-a-bitching side wall is sound proof!'

However, Jack was aware that the situation was too urgent for him to waste even a few seconds in silent self-recrimination over having failed to take such a point into consideration!

Shoving the girls onwards, with instructions in Spanish — which he knew would be more easily assimilated under the circumstances than words in what was, despite their having been born and raised in Texas, a second language — the Sheriff spun around. As he was completing the turn and starting to move towards the connecting door, he studied what was happening elsewhere.

Having been caught, swung and flung aside by his unexpected assailant, Cleverly was being brought to a halt by crashing against the front wall. Unfortunately, the shock of the completely unanticipated attack had not caused him to release the carbine. Nor did the impact of his shoulders as they rammed against the solid planks from which the structure was manufactured have any greater success, and the weapon remained in his hands. For all that, having contrived to keep himself armed availed him nothing.

Even as the natural instinct for self-preservation — spurred into motion by raw fear mingled with rage induced via narcotics — was causing the blond radical to raise the weapon, Garrity hurtled across the garage towards him. Before he could complete its alignment, a huge black hand slapped the Armalite aside and sent it spinning from his grasp with no more apparent difficulty than removing a toy from the hands of a frightened child. Then the burly patrolman took him by the throat and hurled him aside once more.

That was all the Sheriff had time to see!

Arriving at the connecting door, Jack devoted all his attention to what he knew must be done!

Standing with his back to the wall and hoping it would be proof against bullets as well as sound, the Sheriff reached around to grasp and turn the knob. A tug caused the door to swing open again. No shots were fired and, right hand dipping, he plunged through. Despite Garrity having been presented with an opportunity to tackle Cleverly bare-handed, he doubted whether he would be equally successful in avoiding the need to employ a firearm.

Coinciding with the rapid entrance he was making, the Sheriff enfolded the thumb, second, third and fourth fingers about the carefully shaped, hand filling wooden 'combat stocks' of the Smith & Wesson Model 57 .41 Magnum revolver's butt. Hooking beneath the restraining strap while the rest were obtaining their hold, the right forefinger separated the 'male' and 'female' portions of the press-stud. Sweeping out the liberated weapon with the easy facility offered by the excellent design of the Bianchi rig, he held it ready to be used by the time he had crossed the threshold. However, for all the urgency of the situation, his well trained reflexes refrained from allowing the forefinger to enter the triggerguard until *after* the four inch barrel had cleared the lip of the holster and the muzzle was directed away from his body.[1]

One brief and sweeping glance taken by Jack as he was entering the sitting-room gave confirmation of the reason he had overheard for the delay in arriving in the garage. The radicals had clearly spent the intervening time looking for the keys which would allow them to use the Cadillac sedan owned by Oliver Lacey. What was more, either a growing anger over the failure of the search or vicious spite had caused them to do far more damage than would have occurred merely in the course of making such an examination. It was, in fact, a tribute to the effectiveness of the way in which the dividing wall had been sound proofed

1. *An example of how dangerous a failure to take such a precaution can be when drawing a handgun is given in:* THE FAST GUN. *J.T.E.*

that he and Garrity had been prevented from hearing the activities of the pair while the destruction was taking place.

However, at that moment, the Sheriff had other and far more important matters to consider than commiserating over the deliberate vandalism wreaked upon Lacey's belongings!

Instead of offering to go to the assistance of his companion, who he realized must have fallen into the hands of at least one peace officer, a single thought had become foremost in those flooding through the over-excited mind of Gierek. His immediate response to the terribly changed state of affairs was closer to that of a rat which had discovered the ship it was on had started to sink, however, than of a noble and gallant fighter against the evils of the Capitalist Establishment. The moment he had had the connecting door closed in his face, devoting not a single thought to Cleverly's predicament, he had immediately turned with the intention of seeking a means of escape for himself.

For all that, the brunette radical had not been in a state of complete and unthinking panic!

Just as Gierek was taking to his heels in the direction of the bedrooms, a disconcerting possibility occurred to him. There might be more of the 'Fascist pigs' lurking outside. Remembering he had already fired several shots, although unable to recollect the exact number, he pressed the restraining stud and allowed the partially deplete magazine to slip from its housing in the butt of the automatic pistol. Extracting a fully charged replacement from the pouch on his waist belt, he was thrusting it home as he arrived at the closed door of the bedroom in which he had spoken with Maria. Reaching for the handle with his left hand, he discovered the precaution he had taken was justified and the need to make use of his replenished weapon was arising even sooner than he had anticipated.

'Gierek!'

Hearing his name, the radical swung around and saw the

khaki clad peace officer coming through the connecting door from the garage. Alarm flooded through him, but the snarl which bared his teeth was as much fear as savagery. For all that, he was ready to defend himself with all the courage of a cornered rat.

' "Something" you!' Gierek shrieked, bringing up the Colt and starting to fire. 'I'll kill you, you "mother-some-thing" Fascist pig!'

Three bullets hissed by Jack Tragg's head in rapid succession, going through the door and evoking screams from the prostitutes as they followed their predecessors into the bodywork of the Mustang. Unlike the radical, he had kept count of how many times the pistol had been fired. Four bullets had already entered the garage and, according to the report he was given on his arrival, three more had been expended on Route 228. Which meant the weapon, having a fully loaded capacity of seven rounds in the magazine and, possibly, an eighth in the chamber, had been recharged since Gierek entered the house.

More than once, in fact!

Having noticed the discarded magazine lying where it had fallen to the floor, the Sheriff realized the radical was able to continue firing at least four and perhaps five more times!

There could be only one response in the circumstances!

Certainly no kind of verbal dissuasion, or requests to refrain, would be heeded!

What was more, the description given by Garrity of the injuries inflicted indicated it had been Gierek who killed the elderly woman in the delicatessen. As it was unlikely she had offered resistance, or posed a threat to him, he would have no compunction over trying to take the life of a person who did.

Swinging up the Smith & Wesson with the swiftly deft precision of a trained 'combat pistol' fighter, Jack knew how best to handle the emergency. With his left hand going to join the right on the butt and supply an additional firmness to his grip, he adopted the shoulder high and arms' length stance perfected by Sheriff Jack Weaver of Lancaster, California. It was a posture ideally suited for permitting *very* accurate sighting and extra control when firing a heavy calibre revolver with a double action mechanism.

Showing no sign of being deterred by two more bullets passing so close to his head he felt the wind stir his hair, or hearing sounds suggesting one of the prostitutes — Rosa he suspected — was becoming hysterical in the garage, the Sheriff concentrated upon making sure of his aim. Knowing the shooting by the radical must be brought to an immediate end, he squeezed the trigger and fired in the only way he dared under the circumstances.

Flying as it was intended, the .41 Magnum bullet struck Gierek between the eyes and, having torn through the brain, burst out at the back of his head. Killed instantly, he was lifted bodily from his feet by the striking force of the extremely powerful cartridge. Although he dispatched the remaining loads from his automatic pistol as he was going down, the first of them having been deflected only just enough to miss its intended target, it was as a result of the involuntary twitching of his forefinger and the bullets ended their respective flights harmlessly in the walls. Jerked free of the dying grasp by the continuous recoils, the weapon spun aside and reached the floor almost at the same moment as its owner.

'You poor, stupid, misguided bastard!' Jack said softly and bitterly, lowering his revolver secure in the knowledge he had nothing further to fear from the brown haired radical. 'What a waste of a life!'

No matter how justified and necessary, the Sheriff of Rockabye County never took lightly the killing of another human being!

Knowing he could render no kind of aid to Gierek, Jack holstered the Smith & Wesson. Swinging on his heel, he walked quickly back into the garage. He found he had drawn the correct conclusion from the sounds he had heard. Maria was holding and comforting her cousin.

Although Rosa was still shuddering violently and sobbing, she was no longer completely hysterical. Satisfied all was under control there and needed no action on his part, he turned his gaze to where he could hear the thudding of blows. Holding up Cleverly with a big black hand bunching the front of his loosely fitting shirt, Garrity was driving punch after punch into his unresisting body. Before offering to intervene, the Sheriff located the bulb he had removed and, as he replaced it in the socket from which it had come, it immediately glowed into light.

'All right now, Joe!' Jack said with quiet authority, strolling forward. 'I reckon that's about enough, *amigo*!'

'Hell, yes!' Garrity admitted, stiffening at the words and, after a couple of seconds, shaking his head as if to clear it. Releasing his hold and allowing the battered radical to slide limply to the floor, he turned to face the Sheriff and went on, 'I'm sorry, sir, but —!'

'I *know*,' Jack drawled gently and truthfully, his demeanour expressing an understanding for and sympathy with the motives of the other peace officer. Then his tone became crisp and official as he continued, 'I hope you remembered to read him his rights before you took him into custody?'

'Well no, sir, I can't rightly say's how I did,' the patrolman confessed, sounding as serious as the Sheriff. 'What with one thing and another, it sort of slipped my mind. Come to think of it, though, I don't reckon a real sneaky legal shyster would reckon I'd got around to taking him into custody as such.'

'You haven't *questioned* him, have you?' Jack asked.

'Well no, sir, I haven't,' Garrity answered. 'I would have, but he wouldn't stay still long enough for me to read him his rights and it wouldn't have been legal for me to *question* him until I had.'

'You mean he didn't give you a chance to read his rights and you had to protect yourself when he attacked you?'

'Don't you reckon that's how it was, sir?'

'*I'm* satisfied and I reckon I can say the same for

Captain Bellamy and Chief Hagen,' Jack said non-committally, neither confirming nor denying the question. 'But will that Robertus gal from the local network and the *Gusher City Mirror* go along with us on it?'

'I don't think we've any need to sweat it where they're concerned, sir,' the patrolman claimed, white teeth gleaming in a broad grin. 'That's another advantage of being black. Ethnic butt-lickers like her and tabloids like the *Mirror* are always willing to put it down to a soul brother expressing his feelings of equality when he puts the slug on a honkie, particularly one who looks like he could be a blond haired W.A.S.P. So I reckon they'll excuse me for doing it.'

'Then it looks as if we've nothing to worry about from them, even if they should be riled over "Operation Gob-Stopper" delaying them getting out here,' the Sheriff asserted, being equally cognizant of the advantages offered in such a situation by the willingness of the "liberals" in the media to gloss over any form of hostile or anti-social behaviour by a member of an acceptable "ethnic minority". 'What say you and I head on down and tell those fellers on Route 228 they can come and start cleaning up after us. I reckon you and I have done enough for the night, so we'll head back to Gusher City and see how you partner is making out.'

'That's a big affirmatory from me,' Garrity declared. 'Only, when I've done that, I'll have to go back to the House and start writing my report.'

'And I'll have to go over to the Office and write mine,' Jack pointed out with a smile. 'No matter what they tell you, Joe, rank doesn't have all the privileges.'

'I always thought it *did*!' the patrolman declared, slapping a big right hand against his thigh. 'Well, learning different and that I'd still have to file reports, I've changed my mind about trying to take over your job.'

'I'm right pleased to hear that,' the Sheriff claimed. 'Because I'm way too old and lazy to be starting to look for a honest way of earning my living.'

Case Two
A voice from the past

As the author has good reason to know from personal experience as a member of the British Army, there are few more startling and unnerving sounds than that caused by a rifle bullet passing close above one's head!

The sudden, eerie and, seemingly, exceptionally vicious 'splat!' of the swiftly moving piece of lead splitting the air, *followed* by the more distant detonation of the powder charge in the case of the cartridge,[1] is disturbing enough when it is happening merely as the result of a carefully aimed shot sent *over* a soldier during training for battle and without any intention of *hitting* him.

Nor is the effect any less alarming when the sound occurs unexpectedly to a veteran peace officer in Texas!

Probably, because practical experience is likely to have taught such an individual exactly how dangerous a situation may be portended by the sound, the sense of perturbation it causes is even worse!

Under such conditions, the odds are greatly in favour of somebody trying to kill the peace officer instead of merely seeking to improve steadiness when being fired upon!

An incident of the kind under discussion occurred to Jack Tragg, the Sheriff of Rockabye County, as he was

1. *The velocity of a bullet from a modern rifle — even the far from excessively powered No. 4 Mark 1*, which was the standard issue to the British Army while we were doing our recruit training with the Rifle Brigade — is sufficiently high for it to be travelling faster than the speed of sound. Therefore, it passes the person at whom it is directed before the detonation of the cartridge is heard. J.T.E.*

strolling with his dog, Cousin Ian, by his left knee along the sidewalk of Beaumont Street in what the Gusher City Police Department referred to as the 'Business Division'.

At that moment, however, there was nothing in the outwards appearance presented by Jack to indicate he was a peace officer of any kind, much less the Sheriff — therefore, the senior law enforcement official — of a county in West Texas.

Tilted back slightly on his head of close cropped black hair, the hat worn by Jack was a cream coloured Resistol 'Beaver 100' with a four inch brim and its 'regular height' crown — encircled by a medium width dark green, rusty red and deep blue feather band — fashioned in a 'Luskey roll' crease indicative of it having been purchased and styled at the Gusher City branch of what could proudly claim to be, 'Texas's Leading Western Stores Since 1919'. His lightweight two-piece suit was oak brown and excellently tailored. Hanging open, the single breasted jacket had a white arrowhead motif on its pockets. Rolled and padded to supply the sturdiness it required, his waist belt was two inches wide. It had a natural tan floral design on a 'hammered' brown background and was secured by a large sterling silver oval buckle embossed with his initials. His shirt was a dark tan Luskey Shantung, with a shield-shaped Navajo silver and turquoise bola tie. The well creased legs of his trousers hung outside the tops of sorrel coloured Tony Lama 'Corral Goat' boots, of the traditional 'cowboy' pattern except for the toes which were wide and rounded and the heels which were equally suited for walking or riding.

As he was not wearing his gold and silver six pointed star insignia of office anywhere in view, the Sheriff might have been no more than a fairly wealthy resident of Gusher City taking his dog for an evening stroll. Despite his jacket being open, there was no sign of another item he was carrying upon his person which, if it had been in sight, would have indicated he was in all probability a peace officer of some kind. On the other hand, regardless of his attire suggesting some affluence, even if he had not been identified as the 'Super Heat' of Rockabye County it was unlikely any criminal would have considered him a suitable and easy candidate for a mugging or other kind of robbery.

In addition to the aura of hard and powerful physical strength Jack exuded, even without trying, the dog which was accompanying him — needing no lead to keep it at the 'heel' position — would have served as a further deterrent. Such a high standard of training was only rarely restricted to instilling nothing more than obedience. On the other hand, although it was most competent at tracking and attack work,[2] it was not one of the breeds which were usually employed for 'police' duties in the United States.

Red wheaten in colour, Cousin Ian stood a good twenty-seven inches at the shoulder and weighed some eighty hard muscled pounds. Like its master, there was not an ounce of surplus fat anywhere on its sleek and powerful frame. In fact, the gloss to its short coat, the jaunty carriage of its upwards curving tail, and the leisurely seeming, yet effortless, way in which it moved exhibited it was in most excellent physical condition. While bearing some resemblance to a Labrador retriever in its bodily configuration, the line of hair which ran — decreasing symmetrically from the pair of 'crowns', facing each other at the shoulder blades, to the top of the hips — indicated it was a Rhodesian ridgeback and a superlative example of its kind.

Regardless of external appearances, however, the Sheriff was indulging in something potentially more serious than merely taking a leisurely walk with his dog!

The matter which had brought Jack to Beaumont Street could even have resulted in the shot being fired at him!

2. *A more complete description and information regarding another type of work in which Cousin Ian was equally proficient is given in:* THE SHERIFF OF ROCKABYE COUNTY. *J.T.E.*

Like all his deputies and peace officers in general throughout the United States, the Sheriff was considered to be on duty twenty-four hours a day!

Therefore, despite having been waiting to act as host at a small dinner party in the condominium he and his wife maintained as a town residence, a telephone call Jack had received caused him to take his departure before the guests arrived. The message had come from a man who had been a reliable 'stoolpigeon' for many years, requesting a meeting to divulge news of considerable importance and urgency. Matteo Munez had also declared the passing on of the information could not wait until the following morning if the Sheriff's Office was to beenfit from it and would only be delivered to Jack in person. Accepting that the matter would be worthwhile, as all similar calls from Munez had been in the past, he had asked his wife to make apologies for his — he hoped temporary — absence. Knowing this was one of the penalites of being married to a peace officer, she had raised no objections.

Taking the big ridgeback with him, to act as what would appear to be the reason for his behaviour while following the instructions he had received, Jack had driven in his private vehicle towards the area designated for the meeting.

One of the peculiarities developed by Munez was that he would never arrange his rendezvous with the Sheriff — to whom alone he offered his specialized services — any way except on foot. What was more, despite numerous assurances by Jack, he had always insisted upon the meeting place being in an area where there was unlikely to be anybody else around. This was the reason Business Division had always been a favourite location when he wished to impart information. Consisting of office buildings and shops of various kinds, with little or no resident population, its premises were at best sparsely occupied even in the early evening.

This was particularly the case where Beaumont Street was concerned!

At that moment, as far as Jack could see, he had the street to himself!

In part, this was the fault of the Sheriff. Respecting the strictures of his informant, being all too aware of the penalties inflicted by the underworld upon those guilty of such a betrayal as was contemplated, he had contacted Central Control at the Department of Public Safety Building and requested all routine police patrols through the street to be diverted until he had completed the meeting.

There was nobody else in sight!

Even the man Jack had come to see was not in view!

Having left the Buick some distance away, in accordance with his instructions, the Sheriff was completing the remainder of the rendezvous on foot!

As he was strolling along, watching the doorway of the shop Munez had stipulated as the meeting place and in the dark shadows of which he assumed the other was waiting, Jack was wondering what could have been learned that would not have waited until the following morning to be passed on. Even with the stoolpigeon's natural desire for secrecy, there were numerous places where a sufficiently confidential get together was possible in the daytime.

Knowing Munez, however, the Sheriff felt sure that whatever the news might be he would not be wasting his time by coming away from the party to hear it. Some stoolpigeons might attempt, by suggesting a much greater urgency than was actually the case, to increase the amount of the payment they would receive. Trying to take advantage in this fashion had never been the way with Munez. What was more, it would have been a very stupid — or foolhardy — informer to even contemplate playing such a game with a man as experienced in all aspects of practical law enforcement and possessing the added authority granted to Jack Tragg by virtue of his appointment as the Sheriff of Rockabye County.

Coming from the blackness of an areaway between a bookstore and a haberdashery shop, both clearly closed and unoccupied for the night, a shot from the other side of the street brought an abrupt end to the train of thought upon which Jack was engaged!

*　　*　　*

'There's one thing I just *can't* understand,' Helen Hughes declared, running a much jewelled hand through her casually yet elegantly coiffured blonde hair. 'With his family being able to offer so many much more *worthwhile* opportunities, why should Brad waste his time being a *deputy sheriff*?'

Although it had been directed at the woman and man with whom she was conversing, the blonde spoke sufficiently loudly and possessed such a carrying voice that her comment reached the other ten guests at the party and made them fall silent. As they were all involved in some way with the local law enforcement agencies, none of them were enamoured of the disdainful way in which the last two words were uttered.

The couple to whom the remark was addressed shared the resentment!

'I would hardly call it *wasting* his time,' Mrs. Brenda Tragg answered, her accent indicative of British upper class "county" origins. She spoke with a quiet politeness, but there was an undercurrent of antipathy which was discernible to anybody who was better acquainted with her than the blonde. 'Being a *deputy sheriff* is a *very* worthwhile occupation, in my opinion. And Brad is quite good at it.'

The wife of the Sheriff of Rockabye County, whose maiden name had been 'Besgrove-Woodstole' and who could employ the prefix, 'Right Honourable' which was

3. *Information regarding an earlier member of the Besgrove-Woodstole family, the Right Honourable Lady Winifred Amelia who — using the alias 'Freddie Woods' — migrated to and married in the United States of America can be found in various volumes of the* Floating Outfit *and, by inference,* Alvin Dustine 'Cap' Fog *series. She also makes 'guest' appearances in:* WHITE STALLION, RED MARE *and* Port Five, Belle 'the Rebel Spy' Boyd in, 'The Butcher's Fiery End'. J.T.'S LADIES. *J.T.E.*

awarded in the country of her birth,[3] was some five years younger than her husband. About five foot seven inches in height, willowly without being in any way skinny or raw-boned, her slender figure was enhanced by the stylish blue and white cocktail gown she had donned for the occasion. Cut short for convenience, due to the extremely active life she led, her ash-blonde hair needed no artificial additives to retain its natural colour. Long hours spent in the open air, running the horse ranch they owned with considerable proficiency and profit, had failed to harshen the texture of her skin to any noticeable extent, having left it a rich golden bronze. She had a maturely beautiful face which exuded an aura of self confidence. There was also an undefinable air about her features suggesting she would stand no nonsense — nor would she, as more than one brash young cowhand had discovered to his cost when he aroused her temper — and who possessed an inborn facility for instinctive leadership which stemmed from belonging to a family long accustomed to finding them-selves in positions of command.

'And I get a whole heap of satisfaction out of being a peace officer,' asserted the man about whom the comments had been made. Something in his soft spoken Texas drawl indicated he considered the first remark was uncalled for and, particularly in the present company, out of line. 'More than I would from *anything* the family could offer.'

In appearance, Deputy Sheriff Bradford 'Brad' Counter might have been newly arrived from 'Muscle Beach' in Southern California, or could compete — probably with success — in a 'Mr. Universe' competition. Six foot three inches tall, he had tremendously wide shoulders that trimmed to a lean waist set upon powerful hips and legs. Shortish and newly barbered, his golden blond hair topped a tanned, clean shaved and exception-ally handsome face. As was the case with Jack Tragg, perhaps even more so, there was nothing about his attire externally to indicate he was a peace officer. Rather he looked like a prosperous young yet senior business executive. He was wearing a tailor-made light-weight, Western-style two piece silver-grey suit, a cream coloured shirt, a Rockabye County Country Club necktie and Tony Lama 'Centre Cut Ostrich' boots. So excellently had his jacket been fitted and cut that, even when fastened, there was no sign of the Colt Government Model of 1911 automatic pistol — regardless of its overall length being eight and a half inches and weighing, even when the magazine was empty, two pounds, seven ounces — in the Hardy-Cooper spring retention shoulder holster beneath its left side.

However, although the attire worn by the blond giant as usual — except when on an assignment where it would have been out of place, or character — clearly cost more than was normal for a deputy sheriff, this caused nobody who knew the facts even the slightest qualms over his honesty. As was intimated by the young woman he was now regretting have brought to the party, his family connections put him in possession of independent means and he was not solely reliant upon his salary as a peace officer for indulging in his sartorial tastes.[4]

'But being one cuts into your social life so much!' protested the beautiful, curvaceous, expensively clothed and jewelled blonde. 'Why only a fortnight ago, you had to call off our weekend trip to the sports car rally in Juarez at the last minute.'

'Like I said, a case had come up,' Brad answered, his tone suggesting he was growing tired of offering the explanation. However, he could not prevent his gaze flickering briefly to another member of the Sheriff's Office who was present as he was speaking. 'My team caught it, so I couldn't go.'

'You couldn't even loan me your MG to use while I was there,' Sheila pointed out sullenly, this having been more of an irritant than the failure to accompany her as her

---

4. *Information regarding the family background and special qualifications of Deputy Sheriff Bradford 'Brad' Counter is given in:* APPENDIX ONE. *J.T.E.*

attitude implied. She had noticed the interplay of glances between the two peace officers and read more into them than was the case as she went on, 'And you *knew* I was counting on winning the rally with it.'

'Why sure,' the blond giant drawled, without any hint of contrition. 'But I'd already told Alice she could have it for her trip to El Paso.'

Which was true!

As far as it went!

However, a more complete explanation would have done nothing to reduce the ire of Helen Hughes, even though the loan had not been made for the reasons she suspected!

It would, in fact, certainly have had the opposite effect!

The ghost of a smile played upon the lips of the person responsible for the dissension as she listened to the truncated explanation. Although she had borrowed the imported MG M.G.B. convertible from Brad for the purpose he described, the loan was actually in repayment for a favour she had rendered. She had completed some routine office work so he could join the Sheriff to hunt down a stock killing mountain lion and, inadvertently, this led to him becoming involved in and kept occupied by an investigation during the weekend when he should have been off watch.[5] However, any sympathy she might have felt for the blonde had been swept away by having heard what she too felt were most uncalled for comments about the career chosen by the blond giant.

While Woman Deputy Alice Fayde could not quite compete with Sheila for out and out eye-catching beauty, she was far from unattractive and was equally well endowed as far as curves were concerned. There was an aura of friendly self assurance, rather than sullen arrogance, about her good looking features. They also suggested, truthfully, that she had been matured yet not embittered, or rendered uncaring, by seeing much of life — and

5. *Told in:* THE SHERIFF OF ROCKABYE COUNTY. *J.T.E.*

death — in the course of her career as a peace officer.[6] She had had her red hair cut and trimmed in a shortish flip style which had the advantage of looking and staying neat, without requiring constant attention to keep it that way. At five foot seven in height, her thirty-seven, twenty-eight, thirty-six inch figure filled the lightweight pale blue blouse and slacks she had on in a manner calculated — although not deliberately intended — to draw glances from men in almost any company.

'I say, Brad,' Brenda remarked, her tone and demeanour indicating she considered enough had been said upon the subject under discussion and the matter was now closed. 'Did your Uncle Beau ever tell you about what happened to himself and my Uncle Stanley one night towards the end of the Battle of Britain?'

'That depends, ma'am,' the blond giant replied, with a grin and a similar attitude, the uncle in question having served with distinction as a fighter pilot in the Royal Air Force all through World War II. All too willing to support the wishes of his hostess, he continued, 'Would it be something you can tell about in mixed company?'

'*This* incident is, strange as it might strike you, knowing them,' Brenda declared, also smiling. 'They, Ian Smith from Southern Rhodesia — long before he was forced to take high office in its Government — a couple of Afrikaaners who had joined in 'Thirty-Nine and David Ramage — he was on temporary loan from the Fleet Air Arm at the time — [7] had been sent on rest after flying four

6. *Information regarding the career and special qualifications of Woman Deputy Alice Fayde is given in:* APPENDIX TWO. *J.T.E.*

7. *The researches of fictionist-genealogist Philip José Farmer — author of, among numerous other works,* TARZAN ALIVE, A Definitive Biography Of Lord Greystoke *and* DOC SAVAGE, His Apocalyptic Life *— have established that Sub-Lieutenant (as he was then) currently Vice Admiral Sir David Andrew Uglow Ramage, K.C.B., D.S.O. and Bar, D.S.C. and Two Bars, R. N. Rtd., is a descendant of Admiral of the Fleet Nicholas, Eleventh Earl of Blazey, details of whose career whilst he was still Lord Ramage are given in the series of biographies of His Lordship by Dudley Pope. J.T.E.*

or five sorties a day throughout the Battle to a town where there had never been any enemy action. Well, they were walking home after a session in a pub the first evening and, understandably, they were somewhat less than quiet.'

'Was I asked, I'd say real rowdy would be closer to it, ma'am,' Brad suggested. 'At least, that's what I'd expect from what I've seen of Uncle Beau, Lord Stanley and those good old boys who flew with the Eagle Squadrons[8] when they get together with the Confederate States' Air Force down to Arlington Field for a reunion.[9] They whoop things up the way I've always read Great-Grandpappy Mark and the rest of Ole Devil's floating outfit used to when they hit town at the end of a trail drive.'

'Very well then, "*real rowdy*", if you will, and with good cause to be that way after all they had gone through,' Brenda corrected. 'Anyway, they were passing this house singing *Dixie* when its front door was thrown open. A grubby little fat man wearing a mackintosh and smoking a pipe came out and said, "I wish you *soldiers* would stop making all that noise. I was up all last night *fire watching* and my wife Mary is trying to write a poem." '

'What did they say to that?' the big blond inquired.

'Uncle Stanley is always a bit — vague, shall we say — on the point,' Brenda answered. 'But he claims it couldn't have improved relations to any great extent when Ian and the grubby little man met in later years on H. —.' The ringing from the telephone in the corner of the room interrupted the story. Crossing to lift the receiver, she said, 'Mrs. Tragg — No, Ric, I'm afraid he isn't here. Can I help?'

Although Alice and Brad were too polite to let their

8. *'Eagle Squadron': name given to the squadrons of Fighter Command formed by Americans who had enlisted in the Royal Air Force prior to the official entry as a belligerent of the United States of America during World War II. J.T.E.*
9. *'Confederate States' Air Force': an organization of wealthy enthusiasts who own and maintain aircraft used in World War II in flying condition. J.T.E.*

interest be obvious, they once again exchanged glances when they heard the name used by their hostess. Looking at her with greater attention, they saw her stiffen a trifle as she listened to what was being said by the man at the other end of the line. The movement was only slight and would have escaped the notice of most people. However, the red head and the blond giant were trained observers. Each was aware that, for the normally composed woman to display even so much emotion, the incoming message must be something out of the ordinary at the very least.

'That was Ric Alvarez,' Brenda said, although the identification was unnecessary as she was directing the words to her husband's two deputies rather than the rest of the guests, as she hung up the receiver. 'He says a report has just come in that the body of an informer has been found.'

'Murdered?' Brad asked, although — knowing the message had come from the Night Watch Commander, First Deputy Ricardo Alvarez[10] — the words were more of a statement.

'Yes,' Brenda replied.

'Mine,' Alice said quietly, having followed departmental regulations by informing the Sheriff's Office of where she would be spending the evening as — she did not doubt — had the blond giant. 'Or Brad's?'

'Neither,' Brenda answered, and only the keenest of observers could have detected the slight suggestion of concern in her voice. 'It's the man Jack has gone to meet and, according to all the signs, he was killed about five minutes after he'd called here to ask for the meeting.'

'That soon, huh?' Brad breathed, then he raised his voice slightly. 'Where's the meet at, ma'am?'

'Somewhere on Beaumont,' Brenda replied, reminded of two good hunting dogs scenting their quarry as she looked from the big blond to the red head and back. 'The

10. *Due to an oversight when we were working on the production of,* THE ¼ SECOND DRAW, *we referred to First Deputy Ricardo Alvarez as 'Ric Ricardo'. J.T.E.*

trouble is, Ric tells me all his teams are out catching squeals —!'

'We'll find him!' Alice stated, throwing a quick look at the other deputy.

'You can bet on it,' Brad seconded. 'Your car, or mine?'

'Mine would be best,' decided the red head, the latter part of the blond giant's comment having been directed at her. 'I can put my gumball on the roof and run "Code Three"!'

'Really, Brad!' Helen almost squealed, as she realized what was portended by the exchange of comments. 'Surely you don't propose to just dash off and leave me wi —!'

'I'll be back as soon as we know the Sheriff is all right,' the blond giant replied, in a tone which warned he would brook no argument on the issue. 'Let's get the show rolling, Alice!'

'Sorry, Tom,' the red head apologized to the tall, good looking young man with whom she had come to the party.

'I know how it is, Alice,' replied Doctor Thomas Harding. Being a pathologist for the Scientific Investigation Bureau of the Department of Public Safety had accustomed him to the loyalty and sense of duty displayed by the majority of the local peace officers 'And I hope everything is all right with the Sheriff.'

Despite hearing how the other guest most affected by the news was taking the separation from his partner, the anger did not leave the face of the beautiful blonde as she watched the big deputy crossing the room with the shapely red head.

While Brad was opening the door, Alice collected the bulky black Pete Ludwig shoulder bag from the table near to it. Designed for use by female peace officers whether in or out of uniform — unless the latter called for something less sizeable and more in keeping with the dictates of fashion — this contained the items most generally needed when on duty. Held in a detachable holster was her Colt Cobra .38 Special revolver, there was also a small reserve of ammunition for it. Her id. wallet was inside, holding her badge of office and a card with a passport type photograph and other details to help establish she was the person she claimed to be. A whistle, notepad, black, red, blue and green ballpoint pens, a small flashlight and a roll of plastic bags, with tags to be attached bearing details of the contents, were also included.

Swinging the bag's strap on to her left shoulder, the red head preceded the blond giant from the room.

'Oh dear, I do hope they won't be long,' Brenda remarked, as the door closed behind the departing deputies' showing no sign of the anxiety aroused by the call, regardless of being aware of how competently her husband could take care of himself. 'Anyway, in case they are and with your permission, I'll tell cook dinner will be a little later than expected. Does anybody want another drink before I go?'

'I feel a headache coming on,' Helen stated, seeing her hostess was looking at her while asking the question. 'If you'll call me a cab, I think I will go home.'

'I'm sorry to hear you aren't feeling at your best, dear,' Brenda replied, with what appeared to be genuine commiseration. However, she made no attempt to dissuade the blonde from leaving. Instead, she went on, 'But we can't let you go home by cab in that case. Tom, would you be a darling and drive Miss Hughes home?'

'Why sure, Brenda,' Harding assented.

'Thank you,' the blonde said shortly and without any suggestion of real gratitude. 'Will you tell Brad *I'll* be in touch?'

'Of course, dear,' Brenda promised, thinking that the way in which the request was made sounded like a theatrical producer uttering the ancient cliche, "Don't call us, we'll call you", to a hopeful actor. 'And I know I speak for all of us when I say how *sorry* I am to see you have to leave this way.'

'Thank you!' Helen replied.

'And that is *that*,' Brenda thought with satisfaction, watching the blonde stalking away accompanied by the doctor. 'Now that *dreadful* young person has gone off the scene, how can I persuade Alice and Brad to take a more *active* interest in one another?'

Although the red head and the blond giant were to become an investigatory team of some competence in the near future — and develop an even closer personal relationship — the reason for the union was far from being what the wife of the Sheriff of Rockabye County would have wished.[10]

*   *   *

Missing Jack Tragg's face by not more than a couple of inches, the bullet splattered him with chips of stone and lead as it shattered against the wall of the building he was passing. Acting upon instinct rather than conscious thought, he immediately dropped forwards and towards the sidewalk. However, while under fire from an unseen and unexpected assailant, he was not defenseless.

It was mandatory under the regulations of the Rockabye County Department of Public Safety that every peace officer in its employ must be armed at all times when 'on the street'. As a result of this ruling, even if he had really been engaged upon the innocuous pursuit of walking his dog, the Sheriff would have had a weapon upon his person. Being in civilian clothing, he was carrying a Smith & Wesson Model 27 .357 Magnum revolver with a three and a half inch long barrel in a Bianchi Model 5 'Detective Special' holster — designed for the fast Federal Bureau of Investigation type of draw — on the right side of his waist belt and concealed by the jacket. What was more, having expended many hours in training he was as competent in its use as he was with the weapon he carried when in uniform.

10. *Why Woman Deputy Alice Fayde and Deputy Sheriff Bradford Counter became a team and how their personal relationship changed is told in:* THE PROFESSIONAL KILLERS *and* THE ¼ SECOND DRAW. *J.T.E.*

While Jack's left hand was descending to help break his fall, the right disappeared beneath his jacket. Its forefinger broke apart the press-stud of the retaining strap to allow him to bring the revolver from the rearwards tilting holster. In spite of the speed with which he was moving, however, he realized his position was anything except safe. The ambush position clearly had been selected with care and he was illuminated by the light from a street lamp.

At that moment, having Cousin Ian along proved beneficial for more than lending a passable reason to be walking along Beaumont Street after the majority of its business premises were closed for the night!

Even before the Sheriff arrived on the sidewalk, the big Rhodesian ridgeback let out a roaring snarl and went racing across the street!

As always in such circumstances, events were moving with great rapidity!

On landing, the Smith & Wesson already drawn ready to be used, the night was so still that Jack could hear a clicking sound which was all too familiar. It was the noise made when a firearm with a bolt action was being operated to clear a spent cartridge case from the chamber and replace it by a loaded round. Knowing how well Cousin Ian was trained, he felt less disturbed by what he heard than would otherwise have been the case. He knew the speed at which the ridgeback was travelling, its evasive tactics — produced through instincts derived from generations of its breed having been used for hunting lions on the savannahs of East and Southern Africa — would make it a most difficult target at which to take aim. Whoever was handling the weapon in the areaway would need to take positive action to avoid being attacked by the dog while taking sight at him.

The still unseen assailant must have drawn an identical conclusion!'

Or heard the wailing of a siren approaching rapidly from a distance!

Either way, whoever was responsible concluded discretion to be the better part of valour!

Instead of even completing the reloading sequence, much less attempting to shoot a second time, the would-be killer started the engine of a vehicle. Its lights flicked on, including a powerful spot. To the accompaniment of a screech from tyres protesting at being set into motion with such violence, it shot from the areaway. Despite the illumination from the street lamp, caught in the sudden glare, Jack was momentarily blinded. While he was unable to see what was happening, he heard the attacking bay given by the ridgeback turn into a yelp of pain as there was a thud suggesting it had been struck by the car which swung on to the street from the blackness of the areaway and sped off in the opposite direction to the approaching official vehicle.

The route selected for the flight might be taking the car away from whoever was coming 'code three', but it was not without danger to the occupants as Jack could see it departing along the street. The dazzling effect of the head- and spot-lights had cleared sufficiently for him to notice it was a dark blue Ford Mustang, but he could not make out its number. Bracing his elbows on the ground and adopting a double handed grip as an aid to shooting fast and with as much accuracy as possible, he squeezed off three shots. Although the fleeing vehicle swerved, it righted itself and kept going, with no reduction of speed, to disappear around a corner before he could improve upon his aim.

Coming to his feet, allowing the revolver to dangle with its muzzle towards the ground and removing the left hand from the butt, the Sheriff turned his gaze to find out whether his dog had been badly injured. What he saw was a source of relief.

Although Cousin Ian had yelped when struck, the impact had been much less serious than might have proved the case. Going into the attack, the sight of the car rushing from the areaway had caused the generations-old instincts of the breed to assess and set about countering the danger.

Not even the enormous English or Tibetan mastiff — either of which might weigh more than double Cousin Ian's eighty pounds — could have met the charge of a fully grown African lion head on and survived. Nor had such ever been the tactics employed by Rhodesian ridge-backs when engaged upon hunts for the species *Felis Leo* in their land of origin. Whether used in a pack, or as individuals, their purpose was to chase, halt and keep the quarry occupied and distracted until their master arrived to deal with it. To do so called for speed, agility, intelligence and discretion. Great courage was also needed, but not the 'charge-in-regardless' kind which a bull terrier — particularly one of the Staffordshire variety — was prone to display.[11]

Swerving aside to avoid the approaching vehicle, as would have happened when a lion charged, Cousin Ian was not quite quick enough. Caught a glancing blow in passing, his roaring bay was changed to the yelp of pain. As he was sent spinning, the breeze passing through the open windows of the vehicle carried the body odour of its occupant to his nostrils. Coming to a halt, winded without being more than slightly hurt and shaken, he was too intelligent to try pursuing the rapidly departing car even if uninjured in every way. Instead, limply slightly on the right foreleg, he walked slowly to where his master was rising.

'Looks like you're not too bad hurt, you fool old critter,' Jack drawled, returning the Smith & Wesson to its holster and securing the retaining strap without the need to think what he was doing. 'But I'd best take a look to make sure. The Boss Lady would peel my hide if I didn't and you should be.'

Bending over while delivering the final sentiment, the Sheriff felt gently at the shoulder of the foreleg afflicted by the limp. Although the dog flinched a little at his touch, it

11. *An example of just how recklessly a Staffordshire bull terrier could behave when confronted by grave danger is given in:* HOUND DOG MAN. *J.T.E.*

101

neither moved away nor showed any sign of experiencing additional suffering or discomfort from his attentions. Instead, it turned its intelligent head to look at him and wagged its tail a little as if expressing appreciation for his concern.

Satisfied his summation was correct, Jack straightened up to look to where a car was speeding his way. Although it had a siren wailing, it was not painted in the black and white livery — the colours being interchanged — of either the Sheriff's Office or the G.C.P.D. official patrol vehicles. However, the flashing red gumball light on the roof indicated it was occupied by peace officers. As it slowed down, he identified its occupants and walked to meet them.

'Alice, Brad!' the Sheriff greeted, as the driver and passenger emerged from the respective doors of the Ford Mustang he recognized as being owned by Alice. 'Was the party so boring without me you volunteered to catch a squeal?'

'No, sir,' Woman Deputy Alice Fayde replied, noticing that Deputy Sheriff Brad Counter allowed her to do so as the senior officer. 'Your wife asked us to come. Your informer has been found murdered and it happened shortly after he'd called you.'

*   *   *

'Poor Matteo Munez!' Brenda Tragg sighed with genuine remorse, as she slipped into a diaphonous black shortie nightdress in the master bedroom of the condominium. 'You've no idea who it was killed him, have you, darling?'

'None at all, honey,' the Sheriff of Rockabye County admitted, drawing on his pyjama trousers. 'Apart from him being way too street smart and tough for it to seem likely, everything points to him being wasted by somebody wanting to rob him.'

Having had the newly arrived deputies pass what little information he had to offer to Central Control, Jack

Tragg had suggested they returned to the party. However, still acting as spokesman, without it producing any objection from the blond giant, Woman Deputy Alice Fayde had suggested they remained until some assistance was on the scene. Knowing this made good sense and was in accordance with procedures he had laid down, the Sheriff concurred. Prudence dictated he had some 'back up' readily available in case the foiled killer returned for a second try. This had not happened, but none of the peace officers resented the precaution having been taken.

With a couple of G.C.P.D. radio patrol cars and an unmarked vehicle from the Detective Bureau present, the red head and Deputy Sheriff Bradford Counter had been sent back to the condominium to tell Brenda what had happened. Waiting until a team of deputies from the Night Watch arrived with a technician of the Scientific Investigation Bureau, Jack had remained until hearing what the latter had to say. It was not much, or particularly informative, the findings having been negative. Not only had the bullet shattered beyond any hope of reassembly, much less identification, but there was no empty cartridge case in the areaway. Nor was there anything which might lead to the location of the vehicle.

Collecting his Buick, allowing Cousin Ian to enter and lie upon the back seat — which had a plastic covering for such a purpose — the Sheriff had driven to where his informer had been murdered. In accordance with his regulations, Alice and Brad having returned to the party, the team of deputies had followed in their unmarked car close enough to render support if needed. On his arrival, he had talked with the two members of his office who had 'caught the squeal'. They could tell him as little as he had been able to pass on to the technicians from the S.I.B. The killing had taken place in a lonely area of a neighbourhood the inhabitants of which were not prone to telling peace officers of any kind of criminal activity they might have witnessed.

However, noticing a telephone booth a short distance

from the chalk outline which showed where the body was found — it having already been removed by the members of the Coroner's Office who were summoned — Jack could guess what had happened. The informer would never call on his own telephone, but invariably used a public booth some distance from his home. It seemed that, having done so on this occasion, he could have fallen a victim of his obsession for security and secrecy by becoming the object of a robbery which ended in murder. As he was a tough *hombre*, it was likely that any such attempt would invariably conclude with him either dead or seriously injured if it was to prove successful for the attackers.

While drawing such conclusions, the Sheriff was far too experienced to consider they must offer the only solution!

As the killing occurred so soon after Munez had made the telephone call, Jack did not rule out the possibility of the two events being connected!

Especially after the near escape the Sheriff had had from meeting a similar fate!

There was, however, no basic evidence to connect the two incidents!

According to the senior member of the investigating team of deputies, Munez had been shot at close quarters. The weapon used had been a shotgun of some kind, probably with the barrel shortened, not a firearm with a bolt action and, if the destruction of the missile was any indication, discharging a bullet of very high velocity. What was more, there were signs suggesting his expensive watch and other jewellery had been stripped from him with considerable violence. Also, all his pockets had been rifled. As was common knowledge, he never left his home without a considerable sum of money upon his person and a number of valid credit cards in his own name. These had all gone, as had the switch-blade knife and revolver he always carried. Certainly, his trust of the man he was arranging to meet notwithstanding, he would not have set out to make the arrangements and go to the rendezvous he selected without being armed.

That Jack should take it upon himself to visit the scene of the crime had not implied a lack of trust in the abilities of his subordinates!

Nor had either deputy believed such was the case!

There were peace officers who despised the informers upon whom they depended for much information which would otherwise be unavailable to them, but the Sheriff of Rockabye County could not be included in their number. Although there were some for whom he had neither respect nor liking, being aware their motives were of the basest kind, he had always treated even them with consideration. To his way of thinking, no matter how unworthy or obnoxious the reason, they were taking their lives in their hands by acting as stool-pigeons and, as he benefited from their perfidy, he had no right to regard them as inconsequential and unimportant.

Munez was different!

Although their paths had taken them along opposing sides of the law, Jack and the informer had been friends since childhood. Not that their close association would have prevented the Sheriff from doing his duty if he had found evidence Munez was guilty of a crime. Nor would the informer have expected otherwise. There was a bond between them which led the criminal to give information about certain things to the peace officer. On other issues, he would remain silent and this reticence would be respected by Jack. In return, Munez had never tried to obtain immunity for crimes as recompense for his services.

With such a rapport between them, even though it was only suspected by the other members of the Sheriff's Office and they never mentioned it outside their exclusive number, the two deputies could understand why their superior was taking an interest in the murder of Munez. They also noticed he did not attempt to direct their activities, nor offer suggestions which — due to his out ranking them — were really orders. Having learned what there was to know and supplied such details as he considered would help the investigation, he had left it in their hands.

Going to the Department of Public Safety Building, Jack made his way to the office of the Watch Commander to confer with its current occupant. Again, this was not construed as the behaviour of an over officious superior unwilling to rely upon the judgement of those beneath him. Probably even more so than the team of deputies, First Deputy Ricardo Alvarez was aware of his close personal ties with Munez and, as a result, felt even less resentment over his arrival. Knowing his involvement with the deceased, the Sheriff was equally cognizant that these might cloud his judgement. Therefore, after they had discussed various aspects of the evening's events, it was the First Deputy who outlined the procedure which would be followed. The killing of Munez and the attempt upon Jack's life were, unless evidence indicated otherwise, to be treated as separate and unconnected cases. Each would be investigated by the respective team which had 'caught the squeal'. The usual routine would be followed where each was concerned.

By the time he had set off for home, the Sheriff knew the wheels of the investigative machinery were in motion. Already the duty staff in the Record Bureau were sifting through their comprehensive files in search of criminals who had sufficient reason to try and kill him. They were also looking for associates who could want Munez dead, and were sufficiently intelligent to achieve this in a way which would disguise the true motive. There was, Jack knew, nothing he could do to further the efforts of the experts. Accepting his presence was superfluous under the circumstances, he had elected to take the wisest course and remove himself.

Making his belated arrival at the dinner party, the Sheriff had apologized to his guests. When the meal was over, he had taken Alice and Brad into his study to bring them up to date on what few developments had taken place. After this was done, the other guests had deduced that the death of the informer was not conducive to a light

hearted social gathering and it had broken up somewhat earlier than would otherwise have been the case.
There had not been any telephone calls from the Sheriff's
Office, which Brenda and Jack realized meant there were
no new developments in the investigation of the murder or
the search for the would be killer who had fled from
Beaumont Street.

Not until the Sheriff and his wife were in the seclusion of
their bedroom did either refer to the case.

'I hope you get whoever killed him,' Brenda claimed,
having taken a liking to Munez on their first meeting.

'So do I,' Jack admitted grimly. Then he relaxed and a
grin came to his face as he went on, 'Hey though, why did
you send Alice and Brad out to me. They said it was
because all of the Night Watch teams were already
catching squeals, but Ric told me it'd been quiet all
evening.'

'I must have misheard him when he called,' Brenda
replied coyly, but untruthfully.

'Don't give me that snow job, Limey!' the sheriff
warned, stalking towards his wife and reaching for her
with both hands. 'I know what it means when you get that
innoc —!'

Before Jack could bring his comment to a conclusion,
Brenda caught his right wrist in both hands. Swivelling
swiftly, she sent him over her shoulder with a flying mare
wrestling throw to alight supine on the bed. Continuing to
move with rapidity, she leapt after him and dropped to
kneel straddling his torso with her bare thighs. She knew
his moods very well and, realizing he wanted something to
distract him from thoughts of what had happened earlier
that night, was using the kind of rough-and-tumble horse-
play which had served such a purpose on numerous other
occasions.

'Don't adopt that tone with me!' the beautiful ash
blonde ordered, putting hands on hips and looking into
her husband's face. 'I was only doing my duty as a loyal
wife by saving one of your men from a *dreadful* fate.'

107

'Such as?' the sheriff inquired, lying still and enjoying the view offered by his scantily clad wife, the flimsy night-dress striking him as being far more sensual than if she had been completely naked.

'Being hooked by an absolutely *awful* young woman. I feel Alice is far more suitable for Brad.'

'And how does Brad feel about it?'

'My dear chap! You don't think I would trust any mere *man* to make such a choice as that, do you?'

'Wouldn't, huh?'

'Of course I *wouldn't*!' Brenda asserted, in tones of lofty and superior disdain. 'Why look at the *terrible* choice *you* might have made if I hadn't taken you in h —!'

The comment ended in a startled yelp, caused by Jack suddenly changing from passive relaxation to positive action. Surging upwards into a sitting position, the combination of his strength and taking Brenda by surprise caused her to topple backwards and slide over the edge of the bed. Grabbing her by the ankles, he hauled her up from the floor. Before she could resist, he flipped her on to her face and, placing a knee on the small of her back, delivered a slap to her bare rump.

'It's time you learned who's boss around here, Limey!' the sheriff claimed, as the wirily slender body beneath his knee started to writhe vigorously. Delivering another whack to her uncovered bottom, he went on, 'And that's for ruining Brad's love life.'

Forcing herself onto hands and knees, Brenda twisted free. However, as Jack dived on to her, the telephone on the bedside table buzzed. Without leaving his position, he reached over and lifted the receiver. Beneath him, his wife lay without commencing the struggle to escape that she had been contemplating.

'Tragg!' a masculine voice said, its accent Bostonian. 'Sheriff Jack Tragg?'

'Speaking,' Jack replied. 'Who's this?'

'I got your "mother-something" stoolie,' the voice continued, with a hideous chuckle. 'But, although I missed

108

you on Beaumont, there'll be other times!'

There was a click and the line went dead!

Moving gently, the Sheriff rose and, one glance being all she needed to know something was *very* wrong, his wife made no attempt to stop him or resume their tussling!

'What is it, Jack?' Brenda asked.

'Either I'm imagining things!' the Sheriff said quietly. 'Or I've just had a call from a dead man!'

* * *

'They've left the key in the lock, Jake!' Deputy Sheriff Ian Grantley reported, at about the time Brenda and Jack Tragg were entering their bedroom. He straightened up from peering into the hole of the door at the Holiday Inn East Hotel to which he and his partner had been directed by the night desk clerk.

'Some folks just don't have *any* consideration,' replied Deputy Sheriff Jacob Melnick, also holding his voice down to little more than a whisper. 'Now we'll either ask to be let in, which probably won't be taken kindly, or go in the hard way.'

Not only the Sheriff of Rockabye County had received a message asking for a stool-pigeon to be contacted that night!

While carrying out a routine patrol, Grantley and Melnick had received a message from Central Control. Finding a telephone booth, the former had dialled the number at which 'Big Red' could be reached as instructed by the dispatcher. This was the code name employed by one of his most reliable informers, who was small and a *Chicano*. Under the circumstances, the information he received was of particular interest. A pair of 'soldiers' employed by the Syndicate had arrived in Gusher City to carry out a contract. Although 'Big Red' had not learned the identity of their intended victim, he had claimed they were only used to make 'hits' against persons of importance. In addition to supplying their descriptions, he had

109

also told the names they were registered under and where they could be located.

Using the same telephone, Grantley had contacted First Deputy Ricardo Alvarez and reported what he had been told by his informer. The Watch Commander had promised to call a friend on the New York Police Department, this being the city of origin of the two 'soldiers', to learn more about them. Claiming that 'Theo' could not have heard of the pair's purpose, or the news would have been passed to the Sheriff's Office, he had said the other might be able to supply details which would help in their apprehension. Having made the connection quickly and been fortunate enough to catch his friend at the Detectives' Squadroom of the Manhattan South Precinct Station House, Ricardo's faith was justified. 'Theo' not only knew the two criminals, but had been able to suggest a way in which they might be induced to answer questions should they be taken alive. Asking Central Control to instruct his deputies to get in touch with him by telephone, he had passed on his findings when this was done.

Arriving at the hotel, accompanied by the 'back up' in the shape of two black and white radio patrol cars and an unmarked vehicle carrying a pair of detectives who had been assigned to them by the dispatcher at Central Control, the deputies had entered alone. Identifying themselves to the desk clerk, they had been informed that the men in whom they were interested had been out all evening and returned a short while earlier. Ascertaining the number of the room occupied by the pair, the peace officers had also been given a master key which would allow them to gain admittance without needing to knock and either announce who they were or try to trick their way in. Leaving their reinforcements positioned strategically to cover them and cut off any attempt at escape, the deputies had gone in search of their quarry.

Unfortunately, obtaining access to the room had not proved the sinecure which the willing co-operation of the desk clerk had suggested might be the case!

While the deputies did not doubt it would be possible to remove the obstruction and employ the master key, they were equally aware of the flaws to such a line of action!

The drapes were closed, preventing Grantley and Melnick from looking through the window and obtaining information to help them decide upon how to act. However, there was sufficient of a gap along the upper edge for them to know the lights of the room were switched on. What was more, before checking the keyhole, the former had heard the occupants moving about. Therefore, should either criminal see the key being pushed from the lock, they would know there was somebody outside, possibly trying to effect an unannounced entrance. In which case, they would take the precaution of arming themselves and all the advantage would be on their side.

'Ready, *amigo*?' Grantley inquired in his softly spoken, leisurely seeming Texas drawl, bringing the short barrelled Smith & Wesson Model 27 .357 Magnum revolver from the Lawrence No. 30 cross draw holster beneath the left side of his sports coat.

'No,' Melnick replied, having produced his Browning Hi-Power 9mm automatic pistol from its Bianchi Model 17 shoulder holster, his accent also that of a son of the Lone Star State. 'But you go ahead, like always. Don't mind me!'

Receiving the kind of assent which was invariably given when he made such a request, Grantley prepared to act upon it. That he should elect to do so was not a matter requiring any debate. He was the senior member of the team, therefore took the lead when going into a potentially dangerous situation. Furthermore, he was the better suited physically to perform the task of effecting the entrance that was now needed. While his partner was dark haired, six foot tall, lean and wiry, he had a three inch height advantage and the massive build of a professional football tackle on which there was not a surplus ounce of fat.

Stepping back across the verandah as far as possible, the burly red haired deputy gave a quick wave to the peace officers on the grounds below. Having alerted them to his intentions, he lunged forward. Dropping his left shoulder, he drove it into the centre of the door. There was a crash, the screeching of screws being torn from woodwork and despite the chain bolt having been in place, his charge carried him into the room. Following very closely on his heels, Melnick crossed the threshold at an angle which kept him out of the possible line of fire. What was more, the violence of his entry notwithstanding, he retained sufficient control over his movements to come to a halt ready to take any offensive action which might prove necessary.

The need arose almost immediately!

Only one of the criminals was in the main portion of the room. While he was registered as 'Philip Thornton' of Paterson, New Jersey, he fitted the description of Francesco 'Dirty Frank' Furillo supplied by 'Big Red'. Tall, slender, wearing an open necked brown shirt with a lace frilled front, matching slacks and socks, he had the black curly hair and olive complexioned aquiline features of one type of Italian.

Spinning around at the table where he was pouring himself a drink, Furillo let glass and bottle fall from his hands. Although he noticed the badges of office both men had attached to the breast pocket of their sports jackets, he did not wait for them to make their identity and purpose verbally known. Instead, he darted a glance to where his Colt Cobra .38 Special snub-nosed revolver in a shoulder holster hung on the back of the chair by his bed. Realizing it was well beyond his reach, he snarled a Anglo-Saxon expletive and lunged towards the approaching red head.

Coming to a stop, Grantley responded with speed and effectively. Travelling with a power which swept aside the reaching hands of his would-be assailant, his right arm swung in an upwards and outwards arc. The back of the revolver-filled fist caught Furillo at the side of the jaw. Spun around by the far from gentle impact, he sprawled headlong into the corner of the room. Although the red headed deputy turned the three and a half inch barrel of the Smith & Wesson to cover the Syndicate 'soldier' from New York, there was nothing to suggest it would be needed to quell further aggression. Stunned by the blow and collision against the wall, he lay crumpled and motionless where he had fallen.

'Peace officers here!' Melnick shouted, while his partner was dealing with Furillo, lining his weapon towards the door of the bathroom from beyond which arose a startled exclamation in Italian. 'Come out with your hands empty!'

Instead of obeying, the speaker called something in the same language which the deputies assumed to be a query directed to the man just felled by Grantley.

'Cut out the ethnic crap, Rossi!' the slimmer Deputy commanded, throwing a quick look to where a Smith & Wesson Model 39 9mm automatic pistol in a belt clip holster lay on the second bed. 'We know you're not a Moustache Pete fresh off the boat who "don't-a speak-a da English". So haul your butt out here, *pronto*!'

'Maybe he's got a piece in there, Jake!' Grantley called, despite having been just as observant as his partner, putting a savage snarl into his voice. 'Let's pump a few through the door, we can always slip him a Saturday Night Special if it comes out we've called it wrong.'

'Don't shoot!' yelled the speaker, this time in the English of a native New Yorker. 'I'm not carrying, men!'

'We don't see that god-damned door opening and you coming out, either!' Grantley answer, keeping the mean and vicious timbre in his tone. 'I'm counting to five and starting at *three* and, if you're not out here by *four* —!'

'Hold it!' requested a thoroughly alarmed voice and the door of the bathroom flew open. 'I'm coming already!'

First to appear after the words were spoken was a pair of hands, held palms outwards and unclenched as an indication of pacific intentions. The stocky youngish man who emerged from the bathroom was — albeit from another part of that country and using the alias, 'Bernard

Reynolds', with the same false place of origin as his companion — just as obviously of Italian 'roots'. He had on a multi coloured sports shirt, light blue slacks with an unfastened belt and the zip of the fly open, and was barefoot.

'Cool it, men!' Dominic Rossi almost yelped, after glancing to where Furillo still sprawled unmoving in the corner. 'I was only pulling my pants up and didn't even take time to wipe my arse. What's with you, anyways, busting in on "Phil" and me like this?'

'Fasten your zip and buckle the belt,' Melnick ordered, without offering to answer the question, as he reached behind him beneath his sports coat with his left hand and extracted his handcuffs. 'Then get your hands behind your back.'

'Whatever you say,' the New Yorker assented, being too wise to disobey. 'But I hope you know what you're doing.'

'We've a notion,' the slimmer Deputy declared, watching his instructions being carried out.

'But what've we *supposed* to have done?' Rossi wanted to know, as his wrists were secured by the handcuffs behind his back.

'I don't know how it is in the Big Apple,' Grantley growled, closing the door after checking that nobody had heard and was coming to investigate the disturbance. 'But down here trying to waste *anybody* is considered against the law and that goes double when it's the Sheriff you're trying to waste.'

'The *Sheriff*?' Rossi repeated, staring at the red head as if unable to credit what he had heard. 'Like hell we tried to waste *him*. We're here after —!'

'Who?' Melnick inquired, straightening up after having fastened the wrists of the second gangster with the handcuffs supplied by his partner.

'I've got a right to make a phone call!' the New Yorker claimed.

'Only if we arrest you, *wop*,' Grantley pointed out in a savage snarl, holstering his Smith & Wesson to replace it

114

with a leather-wrapped sap taken from his hip pocket. Tapping the new weapon almost pensively against his left palm as he spoke, he continued, 'Only we haven't arrested you yet. Have we, Jake?'

'I've never heard you read him his rights, Ian,' Melnick asserted. 'Did you hear me read them for him?'

'No,' the red haired deputy admitted. 'Which means he's not arrested, so he don't have the right to make any god-damned phone call until he is.'

'You going to tell us who you're here after?' the slimmer peace officer asked.

'I don't know what —!' Rossi commenced.

'Then we'll figure we're right and it's the Sheriff,' Melnick stated, sounding and looking sadistic. 'Let's take him and the other yoyo along, Ian. We can get ourselves in good with Super Heat and make some money doing it.'

'We can both stand to get in good with *him*,' Grantley said sombrely. 'But how do we make the bread doing it?'

'When the word they headed here was passed from Manhattan South,' Melnick replied, paying no discernible attention to Rossi, or the other gangster who was groaning his way back to consciousness. 'The Watch Commander said he was told these yoyos wasted Bucky Blue —!'

'If that lying, bald-headed bastard, Ko —!' the New Yorker commenced, but relapsed into silence as he realized he was being indiscrete. 'I want to call a lawyer.'

'*If* we book you,' Melnick promised, but his attitude implied this would not be done any too quickly if at all. 'Anyways, the soul brothers of that super-fly nigger have spread the word to all the other Third World crap they deal with to get this pair. If we take them to Joey Upetangi[12] in the Bad Bit, he'll lay some heavy bread on us for doing it.'

'Hell, yes!' Grantley agreed. 'And Jack Tragg won't ask too many questions on how come they got carved with

---

12. *We know of no nation in Africa which uses the name, 'Upetangi', so suspect it was created by its user to place emphasis upon his ethnic 'roots'. J.T.E.*

115

Harlem sunsets when he hears they're the yoyos who tried to stiff him.'

'Let's haul them down there then,' Melnick suggested. 'I can use some bread to pay off a couple of markers.'

Having stared from one peace officer to the other all the time they were speaking, Rossi was drawing conclusions he found distinctly alarming!

Nothing the New Yorker had heard, or deduced, led him to assume his captors might be bluffing.

The pair were dressed in sports coats, open necked shirts, flannel slacks and shoes which had clearly been bought 'off the peg' from a chain store such as J.C. Penney, and were definitely not hand tailored. However, that alone could not be regarded as verification of them being so honest they were compelled to live solely upon their earnings as deputy sheriffs. A smart peace officer who was 'on the take' did not exhibit signs of affluence beyond his normal means.

The scowling red head had the look of a hard-nosed 'bull', the kind who derived pleasure from mistreating prisoners. What was more, television series and movies of the past few years had conditioned Rossi to believe that every peace officer with a Southern accent was brutal, sadistic and corruptible. To have fallen into the hands of one was a most disturbing sensation, even for a 'soldier' under the protection offered by serving the Syndicate. Such a man would not hesitate before turning over prisoners to vengeance seeking enemies in the underworld if there was money in it, particularly as this could be done without arousing awkward questions from his superiors.

Despite sounding like a Texan, there was a timbre in his voice and a suggestion in his features of the second 'badge', indicating he had Hebraic 'roots'. However, this gave the New Yorker no comfort. He was aware that, while no movie or television series would dare suggest such a thing, the qualities he suspected the burly red head of possessing were not restricted solely to white Anglo-Saxon Protestants. Past experiences had taught him there were

116

peace officers belonging to 'acceptable' religious or ethnic 'minority groups' who behaved just as viciously and were as corruptible as any W.A.S.P. character created by a Hollywood 'liberal'. Therefore, he considered the leaner deputy was just as capable of handing over himself and Furillo to the associates of the Harlem gang leader whom they had killed on orders from their superiors in the Syndicate.

Furthermore, having made the capture, there was nothing to prevent the pair putting their threat into effect!

With the possible exception of the desk clerk, who would in all probability be compelled to remain silent about the visit — or could be persuaded that these guests had proven to be innocent and had fled at the conclusion of the interview — there was nobody close by. The rooms on either side were unoccupied, business at the hotel being very slack that night.[13] Nor had anybody come to find out what the commotion had been. Therefore, the deputies could remove their captives without being seen or heard and could later deny this had been done. They could prevent any outcry on leaving, either by gagging the prisoners or with blows from the saps each had produced on holstering their handguns, then deny all knowledge on reporting to their superiors.

'Hey, men!' Rossi gasped, reaching a decision. 'Can we make a deal?'

'What kind of deal?' Grantley inquired, sounding as if he doubted the other had anything worthwhile to offer.

'We've got bread —!' the New Yorker began.

'Not as much as we could get from Joey Upetangi,' Melnick asserted in a disinterested fashion.

13. *The lack of trade had been taken into account by Deputy Sheriffs Ian Grantley and Jacob Melnick when deciding how they would deal with the situation which brought them to the Gusher City Holiday Inn East Hotel. Knowing they would be in contention against a pair of exceptionally dangerous criminals, they had been relieved to learn the rooms all around were unoccupied as this had made their task much easier. J.T.E.*

117

'Maybe not,' Rossi admitted, concluding he must offer some more suitable inducement. 'But I'll throw in something which'll put you in real good with your boss.'

'Put it on the line,' Grantley instructed. 'And make it quick!'

'I told you we're not here gunning for the Sheriff!' Rossi obliged, darting nervous glances from one peace officer to the other and back. 'But the guy we're after *is*!'

'You're snowing us again!' Melnick growled, showing signs of impatience.

'Like hell I am!' Rossi protested in alarm. 'On my mother's life, it's the truth. We've been sent out to find the Crazy Doc and waste him.'

' "Crazy Doc"?' Grantley challenged.

'Sure!' the New Yorker confirmed. 'Maybe you've never heard of him out here in the st — Crazy Doc Christopher.'

'We've heard of *him*, all right,' Melnick declared, in a manner indicating the "hearing" was not of a pleasant nature. 'Even if we are out here in "the sticks". Fact being, it was the Sheriff who caught on to his extra-circular games and sent him to the slammer.'

Which was true enough!

A vociferous exponent of 'socialized medicine', frequently pointing to the benefits offered — if rarely fulfilled, although this was *never* mentioned — by the British National Health system, Anthony 'Crazy Doc' Christopher had supported the bizarre tastes which created his nickname by performing abortions, treating wounded criminals without reporting the injuries to the authorities as required by law, and supplying information enabling shipments of narcotics intended for hospitals or medical research facilities to be hijacked. That he had evaded justice for so long was attributable to his having strong connections with the Syndicate. While he had not indulged in any of those nefarious activities in Rockabye County, the parents of a boy he had raped at a party, following one of his speeches in support of socialized medicine. — on the itinerary of a nation-wide tour he was making — had reported the matter to the authorities. The high-priced trial lawyer supplied by the organization sponsoring his travels had failed to save him from a prison sentence, or being 'struck off' by the American Medical Association, but was able to have him incarcerated at an easy going penal institute outside Rockabye County. It was known he had developed a paranoic hatred of Sheriff Jack Tragg, who had handled the investigation resulting in his arrest personally, making repeated threats of vengeance.

However, when Christopher had taken advantage of the lax conditions at the State Prison Farm at Jonestown which he was assigned, and escaped,[14] he had not made any attempt to carry out his threats. Instead, he had fled and was next heard of when arrested for a similar offense, this time ending in the death of his victim, at Providence, Rhode Island. Due to the gravity of the latest crime, the authorities in Rhode Island had refused a request made from Texas for his extradition. For a second time, 'strings had been pulled' which led to him being held in a much less secure penal establishment than his activites warranted and he had once more made the most of his opportunities.

'Only we know this is another snow-job!' Grantley claimed coldly. 'He wasn't so lucky when he split from the pokey in Rhode Island and got himself burned to death in a car smash-up.'

'That's what *everybody* thought!' Rossi admitted. 'But it comes out he'd wasted a hitch-hiker he'd picked up and left the stiff in the heap, setting it off to burn him until there was no way anybody could tell the difference.'

'Don't try to tell us the hitch-hiker was the "Godfather's" favourite grandson!' Melnick warned.

'No!' the New Yorker replied and, glancing at his companion — who had recovered sufficiently to listen to the

14. *How somebody else took advantage of the lax conditions at this particular State Prison Farm, which we call 'Jonestown' for obvious reasons, is given in:* THE JUSTICE OF COMPANY 'Z'. *J.T.E.*

conversation — and, receiving a confirmatory nod in return, went on, 'He went to one of our safe houses to hide out until the heat cooled, then blew away the folks's run it when he left. I tell you, that crazy son-of-a-bitch is still very much alive and kicking.'

At that moment, heavy footsteps sounded on the verandah and the sound of a voice, its timbre suggestive of much liquor having been consumed, came to the men in the room. While the tune was the old cowhand ballad, *'Red River Valley'*, it was clear the singer was making up his own words.

'Oh we-sh got a call from Shen-Consh,

Saying you-sh call ole Big Red right away,

'Cause he'sh got shomething import — imporshant to shay!'

'Keep these yoyos cool, Ian,' Melnick requested. 'I'll go and quiet him down.'

'Yo!' Grantley concurred, then swept the criminals with his scowling gaze. 'If either of you lets out a peep, I'll bend your skulls in with "Lil Billy" here!'

Accepting the warning as valid, Rossi and Furillo did not make a sound during the brief absence of the slimmer deputy. Instead, they listened to him asking the singer to 'Hold the noise down, *amigo*, there's a sick feller in this room'. On being obeyed and the footsteps continuing along the verandah without any musical accompaniment, he returned to the room.

'It's about time you checked in, isn't it, Ian?' Melnick inquired, closing the door.

'Sure, Jake, the Watch Commander's probably busting a gut trying to get us on the horn, *trusting* us the way he does,' the red headed peace officer assented. Crossing the room, he picked up the receiver of the telephone and dialled a number, saying, 'That you, B.R.?' Having listened to the person on the other end of the line, he said, 'Thanks, it'll come the usual way.' Hanging up, he turned around and continued, 'Well, what do you know about *that*, Jake?'

'What?' Melnick asked.

'Seems this yoyo's been telling us the truth,' Grantley explained, strolling towards Rossi and reaching into the opposite side pocket to which he had returned the sap. 'At least, they've been making the rounds spreading the word for anybody who saw Crazy Doc to let them know straight away.'

'It could have been a bluff,' Melnick pointed out, then gave a shrug and corrected the theory. 'Naw! If that was their game, they'd have picked somebody we didn't think was dead. Anyway, we've got nothing to hold them on.'

'Trouble being,' Grantley growled. 'I don't take to the notion of having a couple of out-of-town pistols roaming the streets, it could get us a bad name.'

'I'll tell you what we'll do, Ian,' Melnick said, crossing to collect the two handguns from where they had been left by their respective owners. 'If these two yoyos aren't on the flight to Big D-Cowtown,[15] to connect with one to New York, at six-thirty in the morning, we'll let Joey Upetangi know they're in town and he'll likely figure out some way to move them on.'

'You get smarter every day, Jake!' the burly red head praised. 'That's just what we'll do.'

Watching and listening, Rossi began to suspect he had been tricked!

This was true enough!

Grantley and Melnick were neither so brutal, sadistic, nor corruptible as they had conveyed the impression of being. Although both possessed better clothing, their salaries as deputy sheriffs being adequate for a good standard of living without the need to augment it by illegal means, they preferred to dress in such a fashion when on watch as it allowed them to merge into the backgrounds of the area they would be covering that night. However, wanting to obtain information which would not otherwise

15. *'Big D-Cowtown'; colloquial name for Dallas-Fort Worth Airport. J.T.E.*

have been forthcoming, they had put to use the information passed to Alvarez by his *amigo*, 'Theo' at Manhattan South. What was more, not for the first time when dealing with 'Yankees', they had been helped by the adverse image of Southron peace officers caused via the media; although they felt sure such an aid to the enforcement of law and order had never been intended by the makers of the movies and television series when creating such portrayals.

Believing himself to have fallen into the hands of a couple of Hollywood-type 'redneck badges', Rossi had been frightened into supplying the deputies with what they wanted to know. Acting upon the instructions delivered by the senior of the detectives, who had been asked to do so by Central Control, and selecting an ingenious way of passing it on without the New Yorkers learning his true identity or purpose, Grantley had called 'Big Red' and received confirmation for the unlikely story they had been told. With this received and the promise of payment for services rendered made, he had joined his partner in ensuring the unsavoury pair departed from their bailiwick — there being no way either could be taken into custody and made to pay for their crimes — without delay.

'All right, already!' Rossi said, and his companion nodded a vigorous concurrence as he continued, 'We'll be on the flight if we can get seats.'

'You'll be on the sucker, even if you have to sit on the wings,' Melnick corrected. 'And, should we be too busy to see you off, we'll make sure the Airport Detail of the G.C.P.D. does it for us.'

*   *   *

'God damn the creeps who did it!' complained the man who had introduced himself as "David Blunkett", his New England accent and demeanour redolent of exasperation. Then he continued in a more philosophical fashion, 'But I suppose I've only myself to blame. If I'd stayed in a hotel with a parking lot attendant, it couldn't have happened.'

Tall, lean, peering indignantly if short-sightedly through steel-rimmed aviator's glasses, the lenses of which had darkened to almost blackness in the early morning sun, the speaker had a sallow face with a prominent nose, buck teeth and a chin sporting a dimple which might have turned Kirk Douglas green with envy. The features were made to seem even sharper by the way in which his ears were flat against the sides of his head. As he had explained when presenting himself to the peace officers who came in answer to his summons via Central Control, an illness as a child caused a loss of hair which left him completely bald and devoid of eyebrows. His misfortunes medically extended to an artificial replacement of the 'cosmetic' variety for his right hand. He was wearing a lightweight grey suit, a white shirt, red, white and green striped tie and brown shoes. The attire was of a quality which suggested he was more wealthy than was implied by his choice of hotels. There was nothing unsavoury about the place, but Gusher City could offer several which were more costly and luxurious. However, he had said he booked the room at the recommendation of a friend, as he was paying his first visit to Rockabye County.

Although Deputy Sheriff Bradford Counter and his partner were not assigned to the case, to save disturbing the team who had joined the Sheriff the previous evening and was now off watch, First Deputy Angus 'Mac' McCall had asked them to make the preliminary inquiries on being informed there was a complaint that a dark blue Ford Mustang was found by its owner to have bullet holes in it.

Lacking some six inches of the blond giant's height, Deputy Sheriff Thomas Cord was stocky and hard fleshed, carrying his fifty-eight years of age well.[16] Shoved

---

16. *By an oversight when we were producing*, Part One, 'The Sixteen Dollar Shooter' *in the volume of that name, we gave the age of Deputy Sheriff Thomas Cord as forty-eight. We have since been informed that he was actually fifty-eight. J.T.E.*

back on his head, a tan Stetson with a 'Luskey roll' crease showed thick auburn hair which was greying at the temples. Although his demeanour was grimly serious at that moment, there were grin quirks at the corners of his eyes and mouth which implied a well developed sense of humour and there was also something about his tanned features which inspired confidence. His brown two-piece lightweight suit, white shirt with a silver bola tie in the shape of a longhorn steer's head, and black shoes looked shabby in comparison with the expensive leisure-style clothing of his larger and younger partner. There was a slight and barely discernible bulge under the right side of the jacket, caused by his Smith & Wesson Model 27 .357 Magnum revolver in its Myers 'Tom Threepersons Style' holster, to give an indication of his official status.

Accompanied by two specialists of the Scientific Investigation Bureau in the black and white Sheriff's Office Oldsmobile car assigned to their team, Brad and Tom had made good time in reaching the address they had been given. On their arrival, after having met and introduced themselves to the owner of the car, the party had gone to the parking lot.

Leaving the technicians of the Scientific Evidence and Latent Prints Squads to carry out their respective duties, the deputies had started the routine questioning. However, while amiable and not attempting to lay the blame for what had happened upon the inadequacies of the local law enforcement agencies, which both peace officers had encountered from people of much more prepossessing appearance under similar circumstances, the victim was unable to shed any light upon the subject. All he knew was he had taken the ignition and door keys with him when he left the vehicle the previous evening, but found indications of it having been used — even abused, if the bullet holes were any guide — later that night.

'How do you know it was driven away, sir?' Brad inquired.

'I've got this habit of checking the mileage at the end of

the day,' Blunkett replied. 'When I got in this morning, I noticed it had made a jump. So I got out and went around the back. As soon as I saw those bullet holes, I knew it was time to call in the police. If it hadn't been for that, as the car was otherwise brought back undamaged, I wouldn't have bothered.'

'We're right pleased you did call,' Cord declared, then looked at the man who was approaching. 'Anything, Ben?'

'There's some,' replied Sergeant Orville Bendix, whose speciality was fingerprints. Gesturing with the container like a photographer's bag he was carrying, he looked at Blunkett and went on, 'I'll have to —!'

'Of course, sergeant, I understand,' the bald man assented, before the question could be completed. Extending his right arm, he continued, 'I hope you don't want any fingerprints from this cosmetic hand of mine. Realistic as it looks, it doesn't have any.'

'Just your rea — left hand,' Bendix answered, making the amendment hurriedly.

'You could have said, "real hand",' Blunkett said amiably. 'I've been without the right for so long I don't notice it's missing, although I prefer to wear this one instead of my mechanical hand when I'm going to meet people for the first time as it saves them feeling embarrassed.'

Opening his case, which was equipped so one side descended to form a flat working surface, Bendix set out his gear and took the left hand of the bald man. After applying ink from the pad to the tips of the fingers and thumb, he deftly placed each in a rolling motion to the appropriate square of a card printed for such a purpose. With this done to his satisfaction, he gave Blunkett a piece of tissue to wipe away the remaining ink. Giving a brief nod to Cord, who stepped forward and engaged the bald man in conversation, he set about the rest of his preliminary work.

The task upon which the sergeant was engaged ranked as a major factor in investigatory procedure!

125

Nor had the publicity given to the subject of finger-prints, even that devoted to how it was possible to avoid leaving any at the scene of a crime, made the study of them any less important!

Although the greater portion of the human body is covered with hairs, most are very rudimentary and those which are fully developed are found on only a few areas. Some portions of the anatomy, the palm of the hand, the *palmar* surface of the fingers and the sole of the foot, are completely devoid of hairs. On these parts appear friction ridges which form different patterns. The skin consists of two principal layers, the *epidermis* and the *corium*. In the upper sections of the latter are the so-called *corium papillae*, forming the patterns of the ridges, between which the nerves of sensation terminate in the furrows.

Examination of a friction ridge through a microscope reveals that on it is a row of pores an equal distance from one another, being the mouths of the sweat glands. One sweat pore with the surrounding part of the ridge is called an 'island', the fusion of which forms the raised line. For the point of view of investigation, the friction ridges were divided into three categories: 'fingerprints', meaning the patterns on the tips of the fingers; '*palmar* prints', being the produced by the palm of the hand; and the self-explanatory 'sole prints'.

Mathematical calculations in *FINGERPRINTS,* written by the British forensic scientist, Sir Francis Galton during the latter part of the 19th Century claimed it was impossible for there to be identical fingerprints. While this has been disputed, upon the grounds that an insufficient number of specimens have been examined to prove it, no duplication has ever been discovered. Even when two looked exactly alike to the naked eye, or through a magnifying glass, microscopic examination invariably demonstrated this was far from the case. Therefore, experts in the matter of *dactyloscopy* — the scientific study of fingerprints — and peace officers in general, if not defense attorneys, were willing to accept there were no two identical fingerprints.

Taking a great interest in all aspects of his specialization, Bendix was cognizant with the history and controversy of *dactyloscopy*. Being equally aware of how defense attorneys sought to discredit evidence of experts on behalf of their clients, he was always thorough in his work. He had found, 'dusted' — using powder appropriate to the surface upon which the discovery was made — and photographed several prints inside and on the vehicle, so wanted to establish which belonged to the owner. This was a matter of great importance, but he had also been seeking something which he considered to be even more vital to the conduct of the investigation.

The discovery made the previous night by Deputy Sheriffs Ian Grantley and Jacob Melnick had established there could be a connection between the murder of Matteo Munez and the attempt to shoot Sheriff Jack Tragg. Fortunately, due to pressure of other and more pressing work, the members of the Latent Prints Squad had not found time to remove and destroy the index card bearing the fingerprints of Anthony 'Crazy Doc' Christopher, as would normally have happened on receipt of the news of his supposed death. If Bendix could produce a match for those on the card in his box, he would establish that the two criminals from New York had told the truth about the purpose of their visit to Gusher City.

One glance at the cards informed the sergeant that the prints of Christopher and Blunkett were entirely different. The friction ridges of the former made circular 'whorls' like the ripples caused by a whirlpool, and those of the latter rose into an entirely different looking 'tented' arch. What was more, the murderer and rapist had regular, almost effeminately handsome features, apart from outstanding ears generally concealed by a full head of trendily long mousey brown hair, with a chin unblemished by a dimple. However, even if they had looked exactly alike otherwise, instead of merely being roughly the same height and build, the differences between the friction lines of the fingerprints would have served to identify them and rule out the possibility of the hairless man being imprisoned in mistake for the escaped criminal.

'What I can't understand, gentlemen,' Blunkett was saying to Brad and Cord, as Bendix was completing the comparison and drawing his conclusions. 'Is why whoever did it took the car away, then brought it back here. To the exact place where I'd left it even.'

'I've been wondering about that myself,' the older deputy admitted.

'And me,' the blond giant seconded. 'If it wasn't for the bullet holes, they could have done it hoping you wouldn't know it had been taken and fetched back.'

'Sure,' Cord supported. 'Only, unless they didn't know they'd been hit, there wouldn't be a whole heap of point to doing it, with the bullet holes to show something had happened that shouldn't.'

'All of which dosen't show me in any too good a light,' Blunkett remarked, but in a cheerful and unconcerned manner. 'So I hope you've found somebody else's fingerprints as well as mine, sergeant.'

'There are some,' Bendix confirmed. 'But we won't know whose they are until we've checked them out.'

'Excuse me, Mr. Blunkett,' said the second technician, walking over with hands behind his back. 'Have you been eating at a drive-in yesterday?'

'No,' replied the hairless man. 'Why?'

'There are marks on the driver's door like they could have been made when a tray was clipped on,' Sergeant Ira Goldstein explained, his speciality being to search out physical evidence at the scene of a crime. 'Only they don't usually have the holders fit so tightly the paint is scratched.'

'Perhaps whoever took it went to one?' Blunkett offered, his manner helpful. 'Could that help you find them, Mr. Cord?'

'Maybe,' the older deputy said, nodding sombrely.

'We'll pass it on to the team who caught the squeal. It might tie in with what happened to your car and they'll decide whether to follow it up. Do you have anything for us, Ira?'

'Either the driver was about the same height as Mr. Blunkett, or didn't bother to change the position of the seat,' Goldstein supplied, then brought his hands from behind his back. 'That's about all of it, except for this I found on the floor by the back seat.'

'Us amateurs pick them up on the end of a pencil, according to the movies and t.v. cop shows,' Cord commented, looking at the empty cartridge case gripped in the forceps held by the technician, having noticed on other occasions how he invariably produced his finds in a similarly dramatic fashion.

'That's what sets the professional apart from the amateurs,' Goldstein asserted with a grin matching the one on the leathery face of the older deputy. 'We do things *properly*.'

'Like making sure not to put our fingerprints all over *everything*, regardless,' Bendix added, in support of his fellow technician. 'Which the *gentlemen* doing the *leg work* for *us* experts 'most always do.'

'What kind of shell is it, Ira?' Brad put in. 'Or do we have to wait for one of the *experts* from F.I.L. to tell us?'

'Well, that would be courtesy from one *expert* to another,' Goldstein admitted, enjoying the usual banter which passed between technicians and investigating officers who were also good friends. 'But, the Firearms Investigation Laboratory *experts* are *always* so busy I'll put my scientific expertize to work and say, at a guess, having read what it says on the base, it's a Remington "Fire Ball" .221.'

'There's expert scientific investigation for you,' Bendix praised.

'The wonders you fellers of S.I.B. pull off all the time amazes me!' Cord asserted, in well simulated awe. Then, becoming serious, he went on, 'Does that mean anything to *you*, Brad?'

'It might,' the blond giant admitted.

Hearing about the marks on the door of the car had started thoughts churning through Brad's head. A 'sixteen dollar shooter' on the exacting qualification course run by the Rockabye County Department of Public Safety, to encourage greater efficiency amongst the law enforcement officers, he took an interest in firearms which went far beyond their use in his chosen line of work. The explanation for the question asked by Goldstein had struck a responsive chord in his memory, but he had not been able to bring whatever it was to completion and had turned his attention to the summations he had drawn the previous evening in the hope that they would produce enlightenment.

According to the description of the incident he had received from the sheriff, added to the destruction of the bullet by shattering against the wall, Brad had agreed a bolt action rifle firing a high velocity charge was the type of weapon used. However, some partially remembered fact kept stirring and struggling to come to fruition. Looking at and hearing the identification of the spent case, he had recollected the half remembered details. Or rather, he realized there was a possibility they had drawn an erroneous conclusion where the weapon was concerned.

'Such as?' Cord prompted, knowing his young partner was reticent about expressing opinions which might prove invalid in the presence of other and more experienced peace officers.

'Even though it missed,' the blond giant said pensively, 'that bullet went by *very* close to the Sheriff's head. The areaway was a good seventy-five yards away, which made it a pretty fair shot.'

'Not with a rifle using that kind of shell,' Bendix pointed out, but in the manner of one expert commenting upon the remark of another.

'If it was a *rifle*,' Brad replied.

'The Sheriff heard the bolt operating,' Goldstein remarked, but could see the other technician was taking the blond giant's words as anything but an over-imaginative suggestion from Jack Tragg's "seven day wonder". He remembered hearing that the young man was proving a competent officer and, being a friend of Cord, he was willing to give the other the benefit of the doubt, so he went on, 'Which sounds like a rifle to me.'

'Can't say's I've seen too many handguns with bolt actions, either, Brad,' Cord confessed, but without derision.

'Have you ever seen a Remington XP-100 Long Range Pistol?' the blond giant inquired.

'Well, no,' Cord confessed and, after Goldstein had signified a similar lack of knowledge, went on, 'Which it doesn't look like the *experts* from S.I.B. can come out any more truthful' than me to say they have.'

'It looks like a cross between a shortened rifle and a lengthened handgun,' Brad elaborated, before either "expert from S.I.B." could comment upon the statement, other details having started to flood into his memory now he had made the breakthrough. 'It weighs three and three-quarter pounds, has a ten and a half inch barrel, fires a fifty grain soft nose bullet with a muzzle velocity of around two thousand, six hundred and fifty feet per second and its mid-range trajectory is less than an inch.'

'Does it, though?' the older deputy challenged, but in a friendly and admiring fashion. 'You're *real* sure it's two thousand, six-fifty feet per second, though?'

'Dick Eades, from over to Hurst, told me so himself the last time we went hunting together,' the blond giant confirmed, referring to a very well known author on firearms and shooting subjects with whom he was on friendly terms. 'It's only a single shot, but with a grip like the butt of an automatic pistol — and a *bolt action*, just like a rifle.'

'And, when it's fitted with something like a Bushnell

Phantom 2.6 power telescopic sight, it's one hell of a straight shooting gun,' Bendix supplemented, feeling it incumbent upon himself to uphold the honour of the 'experts from S.I.B.'. He too had an enthusiasm which led him to study developments in firearms and was also a 'sixteen dollar shooter'. 'Which being, I'd say Super Heat had him an even narrower escape last night than any of us guessed.'

'That's for sure!' Brad seconded. 'Parked at the angle it must have been to let it split from the areaway so fast, it wouldn't have been easy for the rifle to be held steadily out of the window.'

'Unless there were two of them in the heap,' Cord offered.

'There *weren't*,' Goldstein asserted with confidence. 'Two of the bullets went clear through the front passenger seat. They couldn't have missed anybody sitting in it and, should anybody have been, there'd be traces of blood or signs of it being cleaned off and I can't find any trace of either.'

'Then I'd be willing to bet he was using a Remington XP-100!' Brad declared.

'Which is a weapon a man with only *one* hand could use, Mr. Counter?' Blunkett suggested, glancing pointedly at the artificial appendage attached to his right wrist, but the words were uttered without any discernible animosity.

'It could be *fired* one-handed, for sure,' the blond giant admitted. 'And with accuracy, was it braced in some way. But not reloaded as quickly as the sheriff told me he heard it happening, that would take two.'

'*Two*?' the hairless man inquired.

'*Two*,' Brad repeated. 'One to open the bolt and eject the empty case, so the other could feed in another live round.'

'Unless it was held in some sort of clamp, of course,' Blunkett hinted. 'And, as something of the sort was recently attached to the driving door of *my* car, which was taken away and brought back —!'

132

'It's you who's raised the point, mind, sir,' Cord put in, his manner polite yet giving a warning that a denial of the point at a later date could be rebutted by witnesses. With the precaution taken, he continued, 'Which being, maybe you'd not mind telling us where you spent last evening?'

'In my room,' the hairless man obliged without a moment's hesitation or indication of anything other than a complete willingness to co-operate. 'But there isn't any way I can prove it.'

'How come?' the older deputy prompted.

'I saw *nobody* after I went there,' Blunkett explained. 'I didn't call room service, or the desk clerk and I didn't watch television to be able to say what programmes were being shown. In fact, I was so tired, I went to bed shortly after eight and didn't wake up until this morning. What's more, the way I sleep, Big H could come down near to me and I wouldn't hear the bang. So, taken all in all, I can't offer a very *good* alibi.'

'We tend to get just a lil mite suspicious when somebody does, sir,' Cord said reassuringly. 'Only, like I said, seeing's how *you* started this, there's some more routine we have to follow.'

'*Routine*?' queried the hairless man, sounding more intrigued and amused than alarmed or annoyed.

'We'll have to search your room and have you personally checked out,' the older deputy replied. 'But you've steered us into doing it, mind.'

'I've given you a good reason for doing something you'd have done anyway,' Blunkett corrected cheerfully. 'And I won't forget it was *me* who suggested it. Don't worry, I'm not some god-damned soft-shell on the lookout for ways to smear the fuzz. In fact, I'm finding this interesting. It will be something to tell the boys at the Rotary Club when I get back home.'

'Hell's fire, Tom!' Bendix growled, having returned to his examination of the fingerprints 'lifted' from the Mustang while the conversation was taking place. 'We've hit paydirt here!'

133

'How come?' Cord asked, turning his attention from the hairless man and surprised by the vehemence of the reaction from the normally unemotional technician.

'I've raised a couple of pips from the cartridge case!' Bendix replied, gesturing with the forceps he had received from Goldstein.

'Whose?' drawled the older deputy, although he was already hazarding a guess at the answer.

'Crazy Doc Christopher's is whose!' the sergeant asserted, as Cord had anticipated. 'There's a real clear forefinger and thumb print where he held it when he loaded.'

* * *

'Well, gentlemen?' David Blunkett said, his demeanour still friendly. 'Are you satisfied with what you've found, or rather, *haven't* found?'

'Why sure,' replied Deputy Sheriff Thomas Cord.

Having heard about the discovery made by Sergeant Orville Bendix, the elderly peace officer had gone into the reception lounge of the hotel accompanied by the hairless man, his young partner and Sergeant Ira Goldstein. As they had entered, Deputy Sheriff Bradford Counter had excused himself to make a telephone call without mentioning with whom he wished to establish contact. While going to the first floor with the other two men, Cord had satisfied the curiosity expressed by Blunkett with regard to Anthony 'Crazy Doc' Christopher. Commenting it was typical of the lousy state of affairs created by 'liberal bleeding hearts' that such a dangerous psychopath should have been permitted to escape even once, Blunkett had unlocked the door and showed the peace officers into the accommodation he was renting.

While Goldstein had set about conducting a very thorough search of the main room and bathroom, Cord had learned more about the hairless man. However, most of the information had been of a negative, or at best

134

unhelpful, nature. Explaining he had recently set up a video tape marketing service based in St. Louis, Missouri, Blunket had said he was taking a combination vacation and research trip to see what openings might be available in various cities. He had displayed a driver's license and credit cards, but was carrying no other form of identification. There would, he had warned, be no point in calling either his home or business premises. He was unmarried and lived alone, with a housekeeper who attended to his needs on a daily basis. However, he had given her, and his two assistants, vacations before setting out and all had said they would be going away to unspecified destinations.

On completing a search he had felt sure would prove fruitless, but nevertheless as a matter of principle, carried out with all the skill he possessed, the technician from the Scientific Investigation Bureau had announced the room was clean. This had provoked the comment from Blunkett, and Cord's reply.

Before any more could be said, a knock on the door heralded the arrival of Brad Counter!

'I've just got word from the Sheriff,' announced the blond giant. 'He says he'd like to see you down to the Office, Mr. Blunkett.'

'Why?' the man asked, but with more curiosity than concern.

'He wants to apologize for putting those bullets into your car,' Brad replied. 'And to thank you personally for being so helpful to us.'

'That's very kind of him!' the hairless man declared. 'And, particularly as I'm at a loose end, I'd be pleased to come along with you.' Then, glancing at Goldstein, he went on, 'Or won't there be enough room for an extra passenger in your car?'

'I reckon we could get three in the back,' Cord claimed, watching and wondering why his young partner appeared somewhat ill at ease. 'What do you think, Ira?'

'We should all fit in easy,' the sergeant replied. 'None of us are heavyweights.'

Returning to the parking lot, the peace officers discovered that Sergeant Bendix had finished his work and was waiting for them. Boarding the black and white Oldsmobile car code named, 'S.O. Twelve', the three men were not too crowded on the rear seat. Slipping behind the steering wheel, Cord drove them to the Department of Public Safety Building. During the journey, he kept an overt watch upon his young partner. While still certain something was amiss, Brad made no mention of what it might be and he decideed to leave satisfying his curiosity until they could talk in private. On their arrival, leaving the car in the parking lot for official vehicles at the rear of the building, the party went their separate ways. The technicians made for their respective departments, where they would carry out the paperwork necessary for the smooth functioning of any modern law enforcement agency, and the deputies escorted Blunkett by elevator to the third floor upon which the Sheriff's Office was situated.

Facing the doors of the elevator, a double flight of stairs gave alternative access to the floors above and below. To the right of them was the Record's Room of the Sheriff's Office, then a comfortably furnished room for visitors awaiting attention or appointments and, lastly, the men's locker room. Three doors opened from the left side of the stairs. Two bore a printed warning, 'FIREARMS INVESTIGATION LABORATORY. STRICTLY NO ADMITTANCE!', a superfluous warning as the doors were not only locked and bolted from the inside, but had heavy and well loaded metal storage cabinets in front of them. Nearest to the stairs, the third room bore the F.I.L.'s identification without the prohibitive warning. One could enter, provided one kept to the visitor's side of the dividing rail and did not waste the time of Lieutenant Jedediah Cornelius and his three-man squad. However, despite having been created tongue in cheek, the implica-

136

tion that the occupants were extremely busy was far from a pose. When not engaged upon some examination involving firearms or ammunition, the four men kept themselves fully occupied by reloading cartridges to be used in the extensive training programme organized by the Department of Public Safety.

Facing the quarters assigned to the F.I.L., were the offices of Sheriff Jack Tragg and the Watch Commander, then — next to the stairs — the Deputies' Squadroom. On the other side of the elevator bank was an interrogation room specifically designed to protect the users, whether peace officers or suspects, from abuses and false accusations. Next came the Missing Persons' Bureau and finally a door inscribed, 'MEN', female officers having to go up or down a floor when requiring a similar facility.

'How about you logging us back in, Tom?' Brad suggested. 'I'll take Mr. Blunkett to meet the Sheriff.'

'Sure,' the older deputy assented, after looking for a moment at the exceptionally handsome features of the blond giant.

Having come to know his young partner very well, Cord was puzzled by the request, in spite of having concurred with it. He knew it had not been made merely for the prestige of delivering a visitor asked for by the Sheriff. There was, he felt sure, a much more serious and praiseworthy reason. Possessing considerable faith in Brad, which circumstances had already proven was justifiable, he was willing to do as was suggested and await developments. Watching the big blond and Blunkett continuing along the passage, he gave a shrug and went through the double doors of the Squadroom.

'Wait here, please, sir,' Brad requested and, knocking on the door inscribed, "JACK TRAGG, Sheriff, Rockabye County, Texas", stepped inside. He left the door slightly ajar and, although nothing which was said could be heard outside, this changed when he raised his voice to call, 'Come in, please, Mr. Blunkett!'

137

Pushing open the door, the room into which the hairless man strolled looked nothing like the kind of office that was shown in an action-escapism-adventure Western movie as being occupied by a county sheriff. Rather its furnishings were such as might be supplied to a senior executive in a major corporation. With the exception of Jack Tragg himself, nothing — not even the crossed Stars and Stripes and State Flag of Texas on the wall behind his desk — gave any indication of the status in the community of the occupant.

As the Sheriff had been intending to visit the Sub-Office in one of the county's smaller towns, he was wearing his uniform apart from the hat. On Blunkett entering, he started to rise from his chair. At the right side of his mahogany desk, Brad stood in the manner of a soldier who had received the order, 'At ease'. Appearing far more relaxed and at home, Cousin Ian sprawled with head resting on stretched out forelegs at the left.

'Good morning, Sheriff Tragg!' Blunkett greeted, exuding bonhomie, as he started to cross the room with his right hand extended. 'This is a honour and —!'

Lifting its head, the big Rhodesian ridgeback looked without any particular interest at the approaching man. Then its nostrils quivered and, letting out a savage snarl, it came up in a swift bound to spring at him with bared fangs.

Taken by surprise at the behaviour of his well trained dog, Jack could do nothing more positive than send his chair skidding back more swiftly than he had intended.

A startled exclamation burst from the hairless man as a realization of what was happening struck him!

The understanding sent a surge of homicidal rage, which he had always succeeded in preventing being detected during psychiatric examinations, through

Anthony 'Crazy Doc' Christopher!

After his escape from the penal institution on Rhode Island, Christopher had put his underworld connections to good use. Going to a small and exceptionally well equipped secret specialized medical clinic operated by the Syndicate,[17] gaining admission through the authorization of the *consigliere* of one of the 'families' upon whom he could exert influence as a result of information he possessed, he had had all its facilities employed on his behalf. Plastic surgery and skin grafts had given him features and fingerprints which no longer resembled those on 'mug sheets' in the files of various law enforcement agencies. Nor had the services ended there. Along with valid credit cards and documents, he had been supplied with other means to 'prove' he was 'David Blunkett' of St. Louis, Missouri.

Despite having been provided with all he required to make a fresh start, and having sufficient money in secret bank accounts — accrued from his various criminal activities prior to being arrested — to let him live in comfort, Christopher had refused to forget his obsessive and psychotic hatred of Jack Tragg. However, the psychotic traits which drove him to the acts which had been responsible for his downfall revolted against leaving people alive who could supply details of his new appearance and identity. Having acquired certain items which he had considered would help him in his quest for vengeance,

17. *On being informed of the discovery, 'Theo' — the associate of First Deputy Ricardo Alvarez, serving as a detective lieutenant at the Manhattan South Precinct — had inquiries made by the Intelligence Detail of the New York Police Department's Organized Crime Bureau. Their investigations established that the lower echelons of the Syndicate were unaware of the clinic's existence and the 'soldiers' assigned the 'contract' to search for and kill Anthony 'Crazy Doc' Christopher believed he had done no more than burn to the ground an ordinary 'safe house' — a property not known to have any connection with criminal activities and used as a hiding place for badly wanted men — after having murdered the people who ran it. J.T.E.*

he had murdered the doctor and three nurses who were the whole of the resident staff and alone were privy to the secrets. Then he had set light a fire which completely destroyed the building and everything which could have established its purpose was illicit.

Shaving his head and eyebrows, there having been nothing the clinic could do to change the colour of his hair permanently, Christopher had travelled to Gusher City to take his revenge. He had suspected that the Sheriff had learned of his criminal activities from Matteo Munez and, while in the State Prison Farm at Jonestown, learned of the obsession with security despite having failed to obtain proof of his suspicions. Going to a bar frequented by the informer, he had put his theory to the test by giving hints that a large shipment of narcotics was to pass through Rockabye County early the next day. Following Munez to the telephone booth, he had used a long range parabolic microphone he had obtained through a criminal contact — the purchase having offered a suggestion of his intentions to the Syndicate and brought the two 'soldiers' to Gusher City — to learn all he needed to set a trap for Jack.

Killing Munez with a sawed off shotgun and taking the property to give the impression that robbery was the motive, Christopher had driven to Beaumont Street and laid the ambush. Unfortunately for him, the only place suitable produced the disadvantages to which Brad had referred. This had caused the attempt to murder the sheriff to fail. Needing the added support, he had placed the Remington XP-100 Long Range Pistol on a clamp attached to the driver's door of his Ford Mustang. While this held the weapon firmly and steadily, he had learned too late it was too stiff for easy movement and — due to the excellent sight and straight shooting qualities of his chosen instrument — flying as was intended, the bullet had made a very near miss. The almost instantaneous attack by the big ridgeback had prevented him from even completing the reloading, much less trying again.

Making good his flight from the area, despite the car having been penetrated by the three bullets his intended victim had fired at him with the Smith & Wesson Model 27 .357 Magnum revolver, Christopher had driven unchallenged to the railroad depot. After depositing the microphone, loot from the supposed robbery, two weapons and clamp in a 'left baggage' locker, he had returned to the hotel and reached his room without anybody having known he was absent. He had been just as successful when, driven by his psychotic impulses, he had visited the hotel lobby — which was deserted — later and, using his own voice instead of the accent he assumed while speaking to the deputies, made the call to Jack.

Refusing to be deterred by the failure to kill the sheriff, regarding it as no more than a temporary setback and even advantageous as it would cause alarm and, perhaps, fear to his intended victim, Christopher had decided upon his next line of action. Before calling Central Control to report the damage to the Mustang, he had left the spent cartridge case removed from the Remington where it would be found when a search of the vehicle was made. Such had been his complete faith in the changes made to his appearance — cutting a muscle behind his ears had caused them to lie back instead of standing out, the size of the nose being built up, a set of deliberately 'buck' false teeth supplied and the prominent dimple created — he had already acquired the means to alert his intended victim that he was alive and seeking vengeance, and to produce a mystery that would confuse the officers investigating a successful killing. One of the items he had taken from the clinic was a box containing thin strips of plastic bearing duplications of his original fingerprints. He had learned of this particular development, an aid to falsifying evidence, from the doctor in charge and had had some made of his own before the skin graft was carried out to remove them. While a detailed scrutiny under a powerful microscope would show the fingerprints were produced artificially, he had been assured by the doctor they would stand up to any

141

examination by the naked eye or a magnifying glass. Confident he would have left Gusher City before such a detailed inspection was carried out, he had applied a covering to his right thumb and forefinger, then placed the identifiable prints on the spent cartridge case.

As had been the case with Francesco 'Dirty Frank' Furillo and Dominic Rossi, Christopher had accepted the image created by Hollywood 'liberals' — who would have been loudly vociferous against any similar maligning of 'acceptable' ethnic minorities — of the stupidity and incompetence of Southron peace officers. Nor had the acceptance of his explanation, apparently at face value, caused him to revise his point of view. Therefore, he had had no hesitation in accepting the invitation to visit the Sheriff. Rather he had taken a perverse pleasure in the thought of being thanked for his 'assistance' and receiving an apology from the man he hated so much, but had failed to kill.

From all appearances, everything had been going exactly as the hairless man wanted!

Aided by his amiable behaviour and the drastic changes to his appearance, Christopher had been confident he could not be recognized!

There was, however, one thing which medical science could not alter!

The body odour!

What was more, as had been the case the previous evening, excitement and anticipation was causing the aroma given off to be increased in its potency!

Detecting the body odour of the man who had almost killed its master and itself, the big Rhodesian ridgeback had ruined all Christopher's suppositions!

Shock at the realization notwithstanding, the hairless man reacted swiftly!

Thrusting the artificial appendage into the open mouth of the dog and feeling it gripped, Christopher swung his right arm. Slipping his real and fully operative hand from its covering, he caused Cousin Ian to plunge onwards through the still open door of the office. Relieved of that particular menace, he sent the hand flashing beneath his unbuttoned jacket to where a Colt Cobra .38 Special snub-nosed revolver reposed in a holster clipped inside the waist band of his trousers behind his back. It was a rig which was designed to permit a very rapid withdrawal of the weapon, and he had taught himself to utilize this quality with some competence.

Seeing what was happening, the combat trained reflexes of the sheriff directed him to respond by reaching for his belt-holstered revolver!

Acting upon a similar impulse, Brad commenced a different style of draw!

While Christopher was undoubtedly good, he was in contention against a 'sixteen dollar shooter'; a man who, wearing a different type of holster, was one of the very few capable of bringing out the weapon, firing and hitting a target at about twenty feet in marginally less than a quarter of a second.

Nor did the Colt Government Model of 1911 automatic pistol being carried in the Hardy-Cooper spring shoulder holster, instead of a specially designed 'combat' rig on the belt, reduce the speed with which it could be produced to more than a fractional degree!

Going into what was once called a 'gunfighter's crouch', the left hand rising to pull open the side of his sports jacket, the blond giant sent the right flashing under-neath it. Grasping the butt of the big automatic, he twisted it from the retaining springs of the holster. Turning the weapon forward — forefinger entering the triggerguard and thumb easing down the enlarged manual safety catch *after* the muzzle no longer pointed where he might be endangered by a premature discharge — the distance being acceptably short, he relied upon instinctive align-ment instead of taking aim along the sights, and fired in .6 of a second from the commencement of the draw. Twice more in very rapid succession the heavy automatic thundered, its cocking slide going back and forward to eject the spent cases and replace them with the next uppermost live round from the magazine.

Hit in the chest by all three .45 calibre bullets with heads like a truncated cone, the triangular pattern they formed being less than two inches square in tribute to the exceptional ability of the big deputy, the hairless man was thrown backwards. Flying from his hand as he went, the snub-nosed revolver landed unfired by the connecting door to the office of the Watch Commander. Tripping over Cousin Ian as he entered the passage, he was dead before his body struck the floor.

One thing was certain!

Anthony 'Crazy Doc' Christopher would not have a third opportunity to escape from custody!

*   *   *

'There was something about that hairless cuss which just didn't sit right with me from the beginning,' Deputy Sheriff Bradford Counter stated, looking more than a trifle ill-at-ease as he stood under the gaze of his partner, Sheriff Jack Tragg and First Deputy Angus 'Mac' McCall in the latter's office half an hour after the shooting. 'He was a touch too cool and obliging.'

As was the case with every fatal shooting, in common with other law enforcement agencies throughout the Free World, the Sheriff's Office was aware of the need to establish the facts of the incident ready to refute any accusations levelled by the 'liberal' organizations. Placed in charge of the investigation, McCall had had everything examined, the relevant details recorded on photographs and statements taken from Brad and Jack. Conducting a thorough inspection of the body, the medical examiner had announced its face and finger tips had been subjected to very competent plastic surgery. Further tests were to be carried out, the main purpose being to restore the original

144

fingerprints and confirm the belief that the dead man was Anthony 'Crazy Doc' Christopher.

With the preliminaries completed, McCall had invited the blond giant, the sheriff and Cord into his office for a discussion. As was always his way, he did not offer any of them chairs to sit upon and they talked standing up.

'He struck me that way, too,' the older deputy admitted. 'Fact being, I was figuring on having him checked out all the way to the F.B.I., even before he started suggesting it should be done.'

'I'm sorry I went over your head, Tom,' Brad apologized. 'But I couldn't figure out any way to get you alone to talk it over. He struck me as being smart enough to get suspicious if he was up to something and would go dumb on us. That's why I made the excuse to leave you and called the Sheriff. When I told him what I thought, he said for us to fetch "Blunkett" in and we'd see what he reckoned.'

'He could have fooled me, the way he looked and was acting,' Jack admitted, then indicated the big Rhodesian ridgeback lying in the corner of the Watch Commander's office. 'But he couldn't fool that nose of Cousin Ian's. You did good, Brad.'

'*Gracias*, Sir,' the blond giant said quietly, but still looked uncomfortable.

'Did you hear about the maiden walking along the street?' Cord drawled. 'She met this old bullfrog and it said, "Maiden, I'm not really a frog, I'm a prince who was turned into one by a wicked witch. If you pick me up and kiss me, I'll turn back to being a prince and marry you". Well sir, figuring she'd have it made should she do it, she picked up that old frog. But, just before she kissed him, she said, "Hey, hold hard a gol-darned minute. Are you good looking?" and the frog replied, "Lady, if you'd kiss a *frog*, you should worry about that!"'

Joining in the laugh, a sensation of relief flooded through Brad. Until then, he had been worried over how his senior and vastly more experienced partner would regard him having taken it upon himself to contact the

Sheriff. Aware of Cord's prediliction for expressing satisfaction with the actions of another by telling a joke, he
knew no offense had been taken and that all was well
between them.

Case Three
Walt Haddon's mistake

'THERE'S no call for envy, gentlemen,' Deputy Sheriff Bradford Counter claimed, raising his arms until they were extended horizontally at shoulder height and, despite his well over two hundred pounds of splendidly developed physique, pivoting with almost the grace of a top grade professional fashion model displaying the latest creation from Paris, France. 'Being among the best dressed men around runs in my family and I can't help looking just naturally handsome.'

'Sure and isn't that the living truth?' conceded Deputy Sheriff Patrick Rafferty. 'And won't you be after looking out for yourself with such a partner at your side, Alice darling?'

'Why that I will, Patrick, me darlin', Woman Deputy Alice Fayde agreed, in a fair imitation of the Irish brogue of the big, burly and jovial looking peace officer. 'But tis keeping me-self true to you I'll be.'

The conversation was taking place at shortly after half past seven in the morning at the large, well illuminated, ventilated and air conditioned Deputies' Squadroom of the Rockabye County Sheriff's Office.

On either side of the doorway giving access to the office of the Watch Commander was a large box in which, instead of being displayed on a wall rack, were stored the assault weapons for employment by the deputies. These were a mixture of submachine guns, riot guns and rifles with telescopic sights and there was an adequate supply of ammunition for them. In addition, each arms' chest held a cased Federal No. 135 Emergency Kit, consisting of a 37mm Tear Gas Discharger and a variety of 'chemical' missiles to cope with different kinds of situation in which the criminals were beyond the reach of conventional firearms.

Twelve desks — each equipped with a telephone, typewriter, wire 'In', 'Out', and 'Pending' trays and three chairs — formed two lines across the room. Along the wall facing the office of the Watch Commander stood a row of filing cabinets, the drawers labelled to indicate the nature of the contents. At the right side of the main entrance hung the Bulletin Board, with wanted posters, routine and special orders attached to it. As in the days of the Old West, although now lacking the somewhat chilling instruction 'Dead Or Alive', the former were still circulated by law enforcement agencies for the information of their fellow peace officers.

To the left of the double doors, above a small table upon which lay the open 'Office Day Log', was the 'Duty Board'. It bore the names of the Watch Commanders, two female and sixteen male deputy sheriffs written under the Watch to which they respectively belonged. Each name was fitted with a removable board in a slot alongside it, the sides announcing whether the officer was on or off watch and allowing the number available to be seen at a glance. Over the door was the 'hot shot' speaker, the inter-office system by which the Bureau of Communications could relay important messages of general interest around the whole of the Department of Public Safety Building when necessary, instead of being compelled to waste time in passing them via individual telephone extensions.

While his surroundings were not what might be expected by anyone whose opinions had been formed as a result of watching the good old style action-escapism-adventure Western movies, the attire worn by Brad most certainly fitted the conception with a notable exception!

A low crowned, wide brimmed white Stetson hat, its polished black leather band embossed by silver conchas, sat at the back of the blond giant's head. Rolled tightly, a scarlet silk bandana knotted about his throat trailed long ends over the front of an open necked buckskin shirt with fringes on the sleeves. His badge of office was pinned to the left side of a black leather vest. While no longer required to act as a repository for small items such as nails when working on foot around a ranch house, the legs of his blue Levi's trousers had been turned up to form cuffs some three inches in depth. On his feet were yellowish khaki Tony Lama 'Centre Cut Ostrich' boots of the traditional sharp toed, high heeled 'cowboy' style.

However, Brad's weapon was a kind never seen in the Old West. Nor had the type of rig in which it was carried. Attached to the right side of his black basket weave patterned Sam Browne waist belt, balancing the spare ammunition and handcuff pouches on the left, was a forward raked and skimpy Bianchi Cooper-Combat holster. Because of its small size, the Colt Government Model of 1911 automatic pistol was given added security from an Elden Carl 'Safety Fly Off' strap which was roughly pear shaped and had a long tang, permitting rapid removal in an emergency.

Nor was Alice any less in keeping with the clothing worn by the blond giant.

Tilted jauntily, the red head had on a silver grey Resistol Rancher 125 hat with a Luskey Roll crease. Although somewhat shorter, a multi coloured silk bandana embellished a similar type of shirt. She too wore her badge upon her brown and white calfskin vest and her Levi's pants were tucked into the legs of natural beige Larry Mahan 'Ladies' Tall Top' fashion boots. The garments were sufficiently tight fitting to display, without openly flaunting, her curvaceous body. Encircling her slender waist was a brown floral patterned Sam Browne belt with much the same equipment as that of Brad, except she carried her snub nosed Colt Cobra .38 Special revolver in a rearwards tilted Bianchi Model 5 B 'Thumb Snap' holster which also offered security at no loss of accessibility.

'What I want to know is,' Deputy Sheriff Thomas Chu announced, glancing at four other Caucasian peace officers who were dressed in the fashion of the Old West. 'Is how *some* folk catch all these peachy-keen assignments.'

'We'd ask you to come with us,' Alice replied. 'But you don't see all that many Oriental cowboys.'

'That could be it,' the Chinese peace officer admitted, grinning broadly. 'Anyways those of us who aren't going sure envy you.'

'I know Uncle Tom did,' the red head declared, also smiling. 'In fact, he envied us so much he just couldn't bear to stay around and watch us, so got himself sent out of town until we're through.'

'Tom Cord *always* finds there's something needs doing out of town comes Frontier Week,' Rafferty pointed out. 'I'm surprised he didn't take you along, Brad.'

'He allowed it was only a one man chore taking him to Brownsville,' the blond giant replied. 'And, seeing how he out ranks me, I couldn't argue.'

'There's some would say it's a prettier partner you're having, though,' the Irish deputy declared. 'And I'm one of them. Sure and I thought it was only us from the Emerald Isle as had all the luck.'

'Which whatever we have has just run out,' the blond giant commented, glancing to where First Deputy Angus ''Mac'' McCall was coming from the Watch Commander's office. 'I reckon we'd best be hitting the trail, pardner.'

'We'll head 'em off at the pass, *amigo*,' Alice promised. 'Let's go.'

Although the red head and the blond giant were currently working as a team, Mrs. Brenda Tragg had not achieved her desire to bring them together permanently. As Chu had said, Deputy Sheriff Thomas Cord was absent from Rockabye County on an assignment. The previous evening, Alice and Brad had accompanied Woman Deputy Joan Hilton and Deputy Sheriff Samuel Cuchilo of the other Watch during a check to ensure a visiting carnival was operating honestly.[1] On their return, they had been informed that they would continue as partners during the remainder of Frontier Week. As they were assigned to cover the Gusher City Police Department Division known as Evans Hill, where the main part of the festivities were taking place, they were dressed in keeping with the spirit of the events being celebrated.

'Make sure you check out the F.B.I.'s "Ten Most Wanted Men" list before you go,' Rafferty advised, indicating the poster in the centre of the board and made more prominent by there being a clear space left around it. 'Working a Division like Evans Hill, you never know which of them you'll come across.'

* * *

Previously, crowds had always been of great benefit to Walter Haddon!

At five foot nine inches, there was nothing spectacular nor likely to attract attention about Haddon's physical development. His mousey-brown hair was neither too long nor too short and there was a regularity about his clean shaven face which, being neither sufficiently handsome nor ugly, would never warrant anybody taking a second glance at him unless he was doing something spectacular to make himself noticed. Nor could his features and skin pigmentation set him as in all probability belonging to one or another of the ethnic sub-divisions of the Caucasian species of *Homo Sapien*. Furthermore, except on those rare occasions when he donned a tuxedo, with all its accepted accoutrements, for formal wear — even then, he did not stand out in any way amongst others clad in the same fashion — he never seemed to be too well or too poorly dressed for his surroundings. The clothing he invariably selected would only set him apart from those

1. *How the duty was performed is told in:* Part Twelve, the Rockabye County Sheriff's Office series, 'Preventive Law Enforcement', J.T.'s HUNDREDTH. *J.T.E.*

about him in most exceptional circumstances.

Therefore, while Haddon would be noticeable in a district occupied solely by blacks, Chinese, 'Red' Indians, Hispanics — whether of Mexican or Puerto-Rican origins — or long haired and weirdly clad white 'hippies', for example, he possessed a chameleon-like ability to merge into the average background which allowed him to pass through any area having a multi-racial population without his appearance arousing the slightest interest unless his behaviour was out of the ordinary. Even in the latter case, his physical presence made so little impact that attempting to give a description of him a short while after the event was extremely difficult and never sufficiently productive for a definite identification to be made from the information supplied.

Haddon had found his qualities of 'averageness' allowed him to spend all of his life since adolescence as a criminal and, with only two comparatively minor lapses, evade the consequences of a career which had grown increasingly violent and vicious. Not for him the more subtle forms of illicit activity — such as the perpetration of confidence tricks, picking pockets, 'cat' burglary, opening safes by manipulating the locks with technical knowledge, the skilled use of high explosives, or the brute force of ripping apart the 'box' by some means or other — which required intelligence, planning and strategy. A 'lone hand', never attaching himself to a gang, or engaging upon any 'caper' of such magnitude it aroused the interest of the media, his speciality was armed robberies which never netted large sums of money. However, he carried these out with a frequency induced by a compulsion for gambling in which, as he was uninformed about the mathematics and methods of the games of chance he played, his rare lucky winning streaks were invariably wiped out when his fortunes changed, and the law of averages set in with resumed losses.

That Haddon had attained the distinction of becoming listed amongst the 'Ten Most Wanted Men' by the Federal

Bureau of Investigation did not, therefore, arise from his having acquired the status of a master criminal. Rather it had stemmed from the kind of error a more astute criminal in his particular line would have avoided like a plague. A store which he had held up in a small Kansas town, leaving the owner and two customers shot to death and the local 'constable' seriously wounded, had also been a post office. To compound his stupidity, or lack of care in selecting victims, he had caused a fire to start which gutted the building and destroyed all the mail therein. By doing so, he had committed a 'federal' rather than a municipal offense and this had caused him to come into the province of the excellent, efficient and, despite attempts at smearing its image by 'liberal' elements in the media since the late 1970's, generally incorruptible law enforcement agency.

While far from intelligent and brilliant in the conducting of his crimes, Haddon was nevertheless sufficiently 'street smart' to have evolved a successful if not exceptionally lucrative *modus operandi*. He struck frequently, but took only cash or such goods as could be disposed of without needing the services of a criminal 'fence' and he never stayed in any location long enough to become known. By following this system, he had had only two convictions. In each case, due to the 'bleeding heart' liberalism of the judge responsible for passing sentence, he had served only short terms of imprisonment before being once again turned loose to continue his depredations. Since the second period of incarceration, suspecting he might not be so fortunate if he should take a third 'fall' — particularly as he had killed, instead of merely injuring, his first victim shortly after being released on a parole he had violated the second day at liberty — he had grown increasingly violent.

Following his habit of keeping constantly upon the move, Haddon had been travelling through Texas for the past three months. Hearing of Frontier Week being held in Gusher City, he had made his way there in search of the kind of prey offered by the large numbers of people he had heard would be attracted to the celebrations. There would, he had felt sure, be sufficient and easy pickings amongst the crowds to make his visit profitable and worthwhile.

On his arrival in the Evans Hill district where the festivities were taking place, for the first time in his life when not actually engaged upon the commission of a hold up, Haddon felt out of place and noticeable!

Despite now being incorporated as part of Gusher City, Evans Hill had been in existence long before the discovery of extensive oil deposits had brought considerable growth and development to the area. On the fringes of the district, the buildings were starting to follow the modernistic trend of the sprawling adjunct which had come into being as a result of the increase in employment requiring added accommodation and facilities. Everywhere else, the area retained the appearance of still being a small range country town.

The resemblance was even more marked than usual as Haddon was driving through the streets of the business section.

For some reason he was unable to fathom out, it seemed to the criminal, everybody had decided to dress as if appearing in an action-escapism-adventure Western movie!

Being attired in a normal lightweight brown suit, white shirt, sober necktie and brown shoes, Haddon felt conspicuous!

Made nervous by the unusual sensation of standing out in a crowd, the criminal decided to get off the streets until he could accustom himself to the feeling. Pulling up before a small tavern, he fed the parking meter on leaving his vehicle and went inside. It proved to be unoccupied except for a stocky, jovial looking man who, like the people outside, was dressed as though playing a part — that of a bartender — in a Western movie. Although he nodded in an amiable enough fashion, his gaze took in every detail of Haddon's appearance with far greater interest than had ever happened previously. Having served the beer requested of him, he excused himself and stepped into the room at the rear of the counter and, swung by an automatic mechanism, the door closed behind him.

Experiencing emotions probably similar to those which might afflict a hermit crab deprived of its acquired protective shelter, or a creature well camouflaged by nature to merge into its usual type of habitat when suddenly transferred to entirely unsuitable surroundings, Haddon felt perturbed and close to alarmed. He concluded that the sooner he left the Evans Hill district and its occupants, amongst whom he could not pass with his customary inconspicuous anonymity, the better he would like it. However, he was almost out of money. Having noticed, after paying for his drink, that the till held a reasonable amount, he decided to acquire it before leaving.

On the point of drawing the Colt Diamondback revolver from the inside waist-band holster concealed by the left side of his already unbuttoned jacket, ready to cover the returning bartender, Haddon gave a hiss of annoyance as the front door opened and two men clad as Old West professional gamblers entered. However, considering the money he had seen in the till was sufficient to justify waiting a short while longer in case an opportunity was presented for him to gain possession of it, he remained seated on the stool.

Returning from whatever had taken him into the other room, the bartender served the new arrivals. They appeared to be acquaintances and he chatted with them, showing no further attention to Haddon. Having finished their drinks, they turned from the counter and left.

Reaching across with his right hand, Haddon enfolded the butt of his revolver with its fingers and thumb!

Before the criminal could start to draw the weapon, he heard the front door open!

Silently cursing his luck, Haddon glanced into the mirror behind the counter and what he saw reflected by it did nothing to reduce his state of nervous tension!

155

The attractive and shapely red headed woman and the exceptionally handsome, well built blond haired young man who entered were dressed in Western style clothing. However, there were indications that they could not be considered as ordinary citizens attired for the festivities and, as such, even potential victims of the robbery being contemplated by the criminal. Not only did they have badges of office on their vests, although he had not noticed anybody else being similarly equipped, each was wearing a holstered weapon in plain sight. What was more, the firearms and gunbelts were of a more modern and official design than would be used merely as an adjunct to a fancy dress costume.

The newcomers were, Haddon decided, deputies serving in the Rockabye County Sheriff's Office!

Normally, unless engaged in the commission of a crime of the kind in which he specialized, Haddon would not have had the slightest qualms over the possibility of coming into even such close contact with peace officers. Aided by his hitherto always undistinguishable and 'average' appearance, he had once deliberately sought a conversation with two uniformed patrolmen in a diner no more than five blocks from where he had killed the owner of a liquor store during a hold up, and they had never suspected he was involved in the crime they were discussing. On a second occasion, picked up in a raid while attending an illicit floating crap game after having committed another robbery and murder, he had put up such a convincing performance of being a honest citizen alarmed by the effect this might have upon his career, that he had been released without even going through the formality of being taken to the precinct house and 'booked' for gambling.

However, finding himself attired in such a different fashion from practically everybody he had seen since arriving in Evans Hill was having a traumatic effect upon the nervous system of the criminal!

Nor were the words addressed to Haddon by the blond giant of a context calculated to calm his perturbation!

'All right, mister, you're coming with us!'

Such was the disturbed state of the criminal's nerves, he failed to take into account that the words were spoken in an amiable Texas drawl rather than an officially demanding manner!

Nor did Haddon give a thought to how, should his suspicions that he had been identified and reported to the authorities by the bartender, neither peace officer was behaving in the manner which might be expected when they believed they were approaching one of the Federal Bureau of Investigation's exceptionally dangerous 'Ten Most Wanted Men'!

'God damn you!' the criminal screeched, swinging around and snatching the Diamondback from its holster.

Before he had completely halted, Haddon was jerking rather than squeezing at the trigger!

Such treatment was not conducive to accuracy!

The revolver cracked, but the .38 Special bullet it emitted passed between instead of into one of the peace officers!

However, the weapon had five more live rounds in its cylinder!

Nor would Haddon hesitate before employing them to better effect!

Under such conditions, only a person with well trained instincts and reflexes could hope to survive!

Fortunately for the peace officers, those of Deputy Sheriff Bradford Counter were exceptionally attuned to cope with the emergency.

Nor, despite the way in which female peace officers in television series tended to behave when similar danger threatened, did Woman Deputy Alice Fayde restrict herself to doing nothing more productive than giving a frightened scream!

Although neither of them had reason to anticipate there might be trouble, the training as peace officers received by the red head and blond giant had conditioned them to be constantly alert for it.

This was particularly the case where Brad was concerned!

Even before he had 'caught his star' and become a deputy under Sheriff Jack Tragg, the blond giant had received a thorough grounding in matters of law enforcement from his maternal uncle, Ranse Smith and Alvin Dustine 'Cap' Fog. Prominent among the excellent advice supplied by the two retired members of the Texas Rangers' elite — if little publicized — Company 'Z' had been the need for constant vigilance when carrying out the duties of a peace officer.

'No matter how harmless a situation looks, or anybody you're going up to seems to be,' each of them had repeatedly warned. 'Always figure it might not be, or the feller could have reason to object to a lawman coming up on him, and be ready to do whatever you might have to. That might sound all sneaky and suspicious-natured, but it's one hell of a good way to stay alive.'

Realizing that — for his uncle and 'Cap' to have survived their respective far from conventional careers as Texas Rangers — they must know what they were talking about and had obviously practised what they preached, Brad had taken all their advice to heart.

Therefore, although — regardless of the remark made by Deputy Sheriff Patrick Rafferty in the Squadroom, which was always passed when other members of the Watch were leaving upon what could prove to be an uneventful, even enjoyable, assignment — Evans Hill was the most law abiding of the Gusher City Police Department's Divisions, the blond giant had not accepted the situation at face value when summoned to the tavern in response to a telephone call from its bartender.

Being given such evidence of danger, Brad responded immediately and without the need for conscious thought. What was more, while he most regularly carried his Colt Government Model of 1911 automatic pistol in a Hardy Cooper spring shoulder holster, he had conditioned himself by several hours of practise to remembering it was not

158

worn in such a manner on his present assignment. The precaution paid off in that he did not, as he had done at the commencement of the conditioning sessions, instinctively start his right hand moving in the wrong direction.

At the first intimation that all was far from well, while Alice was throwing herself away from his side and reaching for her Colt Cobra, the blond giant halted with feet spread to roughly the width of his shoulders and knees flexed a trifle. As his torso tilted backwards slightly, his right hand rose so swiftly the human eye could barely follow what it was doing. Hooking his forefinger under the long tang, he broke open the retaining press-stud and, having been held in position against tension, the 'Safety Fly-Off' strap lived up to its name. Disengaging the loop from resting upon and preventing the fully cocked hammer from going forward prematurely, it sprang into the air and liberated the weapon it had secured.

Scooped from the skimpy combat competition type holster in a 'speed rock' draw, the big automatic thundered at waist level and pointed by instinctive alignment before more than one quarter of a second had elapsed!

Such exceptional speed notwithstanding, the heavy-duty, hand-loaded, base-jacketed, truncated cone .45 bullet flew to its intended mark. Designed by the acknowledged dean of combat pistol shooting masters, Colonel Jeff Cooper, such a load was boosted to 70.1 on the Hatcher Scale of Relative Stopping Power — which gauged the various calibres of handguns on their ability to produce an instant, one-shot hit upon a human being — and put it third after the Colt Single Action Army 'Peacemaker' .45 revolver practically ubiquitous in Western movies at 76.3 and the 142.8 rating of the mighty .44 Magnum. Vastly more potent than the puny grade of 30.8 accorded to the .38 Special calibre regulations compelled many peace officers outside Rockabye County to rely upon, the effect fully justified the trouble taken by Brad to produce the rounds he used when on duty.

Struck in the left breast an instant before he could fire again, the criminal was slammed backwards against the counter. Rebounding from it, the Diamondback leaving his grasp, he measured his length face down upon the floor.

'H — How the "something" did you recognize me?' Haddon croaked, after he had been turned on to his back and Alice was using her General Electric Voice Commander hand-held, two-way radio to summon assistance.

'*Recognize* you?' repeated the bartender, to whom the question was directed, looking genuinely puzzled. 'I've never seen you before in my life!'

'Don't bull-shit a dying man!' the criminal gasped. 'You *know* I'm Walt Haddon!'

'*Walt Haddon*!' the blond giant ejaculated and pointed to a poster pinned to the wall by the side of the main entrance. 'Hell's fire! And all we came here for was to pick you up for *that*!'

Following the direction indicated by Brad, the criminal managed to focus his eyes upon the printed message. Although similar posters had been put out all over Evans Hill, he had paid no attention to those he passed on his way through the streets and had not noticed this one until it was brought to his attention.

Just before death claimed him, Walter Haddon read:

'TAKE WARNING!

WEAR WESTERN CLOTHES, OR ELSE!'

By the authority granted us from the County Commissioners, Mayor and Council of Evans Hill, we hereby serve notice that anybody found improperly attired for the occasion within the limits of the Evans Hill Division of Gusher City during Frontier Week will be taken into custody, tried by the Kangaroo Court and, without being allowed defense or option, fined to the benefit of the Community Chest and other civic charities.

Signed:

Jack Tragg,

Sheriff of Rockabye County, Texas.'

The End

Appendix One

The magnificent physique, handsome features, blond hair and, to some extent, affinity for law enforcement possessed by Deputy Sheriff Bradford 'Brad' Counter were hereditary. As was the case with his 'look-alike' cousin, James Allenvale 'Bunduki' Gunn,[1] he had come by the former via their paternal great-grandfather — master cowhand, gun and fist fighter of the first water, 'ladies man' and occasional peace officer — Mark Counter.[2] However, his interest in the latter had been greatly stimulated by the admiration he felt for a living relative. Ranse Smith, who had also been born with the family physique and handsome features, had served as a member of the elite, if little publicized Company 'Z' of the Texas Rangers during Prohibition and to his retirement.[3]

Although the family to which Brad belonged was one of

1. *Details of the career and family background of James Allenvale 'Bunduki' Gunn — whose sobriquet arose from a pun based upon the Swahili word for any kind of hand held firearm being* 'bunduki' — *are recorded in:* Part Twelve, 'The *Mchawi's* Powers', J.T.'S HUNDREDTH *and, with the exception of* THE AMAZONS OF ZILLIKIAN, *the volumes of the* Bunduki *series. J.T.E.*
2. *Details of the career and special qualifications of Mark Counter can be found in the various volumes of the* Floating Outfit *series. He also makes 'guest' appearances and demonstrates his penchant for being a 'ladies man' in:* CALAMITY, MARK AND BELLE; CUT ONE, THEY ALL BLEED — *respectively 'expansions' of;* Part One, 'The Bounty On Belle Starr's Scalp', TROUBLED RANGE *and* Part One, 'Better Than Calamity', THE WILDCATS — *and* THE BIG HUNT *in the* Calamity Jane *series. J.T.E.*
3. *Information regarding Company 'Z' of the Texas Rangers and the*

the wealthiest in Texas, having an oil empire as well as numerous other lucrative business interests, he had elected to become a peace officer instead of accepting an executive position in one of their companies. He had been helped to fulfil his ambition by his father, Andrew 'Big Andy' Counter, his Uncle Ranse and Alvin Dustine 'Cap' Fog,[4] all of whom were close friends of Sheriff Jack Tragg.

Unlike the other deputies of the Rockabye County Sheriff's Office, Brad had not first served as a member of the Gusher City Police Department, or with some other law enforcement agency prior to 'catching his star' and being enrolled. Instead, he had received the appointment after having become a honour graduate of the Police Science & Administration Class at the University of Southern Texas and, attending at his own expense rather than it being paid for by the local tax payers, passing with honour the exacting twelve weeks' training course for municipal and county peace officers run by the Federal Bureau of Investigation at Washington, D.C. and Quantico. However, in all fairness to Sheriff Tragg, regardless of long standing friendships, he would have failed to gain admittance if there had been the slightest doubt about his ability to perform the required duties.

Furthermore, since his acceptance and even at the period of the present narrative, Brad had fully justified the faith of his superior in his competence and capability.

As a deputy sheriff, Brad had a rank equivalent to a lieutenant in the Patrol Bureau, or a sergeant in the Detective Bureau, of the Gusher City Police Department. In addi-

special law enforcement operations for which it was formed can be found in the various volumes of the Alvin Dustine 'Cap' Fog *series. Sergeant Ranse Smith makes his first appearance in:* THE JUSTICE OF COMPANY 'Z'. *J.T.E.*

4. *Alvin Dustine 'Cap' Fog — whose sobriquet came into being when he was promoted as the youngest man to become a captain in the Texas Rangers — is the grandson of Captain Dustine Edward Marsden 'Dusty' Fog, C.S.A., an* amigo *of Mark Counter, q.v., details of whose career and special qualifications can be found in the* Civil War *and* Floating Outfit *series. J.T.E.*

tion to possessing tremendous physical strength and great skill at unarmed combat, he was also extremely competent in the use of various types of firearms. Employing the modern combat shooting techniques perfected by such masters as Sheriff Jack Weaver of Lancaster, California, Elden Carl, Thell Reed and, arguably, the dean of them all, Colonel Jeff Cooper,[5] he was able to qualify as a Distinguished Expert on the very demanding Police Combat Shooting Course run by the Gusher City Department of Public Safety to ensure all its personnel acquired proficiency in the employment of weapons. As a safeguard for the protection of innocent by-standers when armed criminals were being confronted, the Course entailed demonstrating expertize with other types of law enforcement firearms in addition to his 'accurized' Colt Government Model of 1911 .45 calibre automatic pistol.[6] While equally competent with all types and despite there being more recent and sophisticated variations of the so

---

5. *For those interested in combat pistol shooting, we can wholeheartedly recommend the following titles by Colonel Jeff Cooper as being very informative:* FIGHTING HANDGUNS, COOPER ON HAND-GUNS *and* THE COMPLETE BOOK OF MODERN HANDGUN-NING. *J.T.E.*

6. *The 'accurizing', performed by the Pachmyr Gun Works of Los Angeles, California, was carried out to increase the already consider-able potential as a weapon of the rugged and dependable Colt Government Model of 1911 .45 calibre automatic pistol; than which no other military arm, not even the* gladius *of the legionaries of Ancient Rome existed longer without any development to the original design. The 'accurizing' comprised of the following. The fit between the cocking slide and the receiver was tightened, and enlarged bushing was installed and the slackness of the barrel was decreased, all of which increased the potential for accuracy. The internal mechanism was worked over to encourage a smoother functioning of the operation. Having the feed ramp polished to an ice-like slickness and trimming the mouth of the barrel each helped ensure a quicker and more certain transfer of the uppermost bullet from the magazine to the chamber and reduced the chances of a jam. Externally, the pistol was fitted with 'combat stocks' which were shaped to make certain the hand of the shooter always closed upon them in the same manner. The 'grip safety' of the mechanism in the butt — an innovation of*

called 'riot gun' available,[7] he specialized in the use of the tried and true Winchester Model of 1897 pump action 'trenchgun' when going into a situation where he suspected there might be gun play. Having attained the highest qualification on the Course, he received an additional sixteen dollars a week on his salary by virtue of his skill. However, like every other 'sixteen dollar shooter', he spent at least that much on ammunition to supplement the official allocation and keep up the training.

As opposed to the Sub-Offices in the five other main towns of Rockabye County, the Sheriff's Office — based at the Department of Public Safety Building in the county seat, Gusher City, which also served as headquarters for

John Moses Browning, arguably the world's finest and certainly most prolific designer of firearms, who makes a 'guest' appearance in CALAMITY SPELLS TROUBLE — *was welded into the closed position and the spur of the manual safety catch was enlarged to facilitate changing it to a state of readiness. A 'trigger shoe' spread the firing pressure of four pounds to give the impression of a lighter pull being required from the forefinger without reducing the safety margin. Finally, the pistol was fitted with an adjustable rear sight which permitted remarkable accuracy in skilled hands, even when firing at ranges generally considered to be beyond the reach of a handgun. J.T.E.*

7. *During the early 1970's, the management of the Remington Arms Company considered the term 'riot gun' was inaccurate and had an undesirable connotation as the use of such weapons was not confined merely to coping with civic disorders. The correct purpose, they claimed with complete justification, was to supplant the basically defensive handguns of peace officers in all types of law enforcement combat situations. Therefore, the Company designated such weapons of the kind they manufactured as 'Police Guns'.*

7a. *The Winchester Model of 1897 twelve gauge, five shot, pump action, tubular magazine shotgun was modified for use in the trench warfare of World War 1. The length of the barrel was reduced to twenty inches, given a radiating cooling sleeve to permit sustained rapid fire and equipped to take a bayonet. The improved Winchester Model of 1912 — one of which is occasionally used by Brad — which has a concealed hammer, was modified in a similar fashion and other firearms companies produced weapons in the same category.*

the G.C.P.D. — worked a two-watch rota.[8] The Day Watch commenced at eight o'clock in the morning and ended at four in the afternoon. Taking over at four, the Night Watch continued until midnight. If deputies were required for duty from midnight until eight in the morning, they would be called from their respective homes by the permanently manned 'Business Office' of the G.C.P.D's Bureau of Communications. The deputies arranged their days off watch and vacations informally amongst themselves, in conjunction with their Watch Commander.

In addition to their other duties, the members of the Sheriff's Office in Gusher City were responsible for the investigation of homicides and some twenty-two other legal infractions — such as wife beating, bigamy, train wrecking, assault and armed robbery — which might end

7b. *The 'trench gun' proved to be an exceptionally effective device for use at close, or in confined, quarters, particularly when charged with nine .32 buckshot balls. One purpose to which it was put was to deflect 'stick' hand grenades thrown towards the trenches by the enemy. After 'trench guns' had been employed and played a major part in breaking up a mass infantry attack, the German High Command — who had already delivered assaults with poison gas, including the virulent and vicious 'mustard' variety — complained that their use was 'an inhumane and barbaric way of waging war'. The threat of the Germans to execute any member of the American Expeditionary Force found with a 'trench gun' in his possession was countered by the U.S.A. issuing a reminder that they were holding numerous German prisoners of war and would know what to do by way of reprisals. The threat was never put into effect.*

7c. *One example of how well Brad Counter could handle a riot gun, a Winchester Model of 1912 in this instance, is given in:* Part Two, 'Cop Killer', THE SIXTEEN DOLLAR SHOOTER. *J.T.E.*

8. *As is the case with members of the Gusher City Police Department, other than detectives serving in the various specialist Details — such as Narcotics, Vice & Gambling, Missing Persons, Robbery, etc. — the deputy sheriffs at the five Sub-Offices work a four watch rota. I.e. Morning, seven o'clock until three (0700–1500); Afternoon, three to eleven (1500–2300); Night, eleven until seven the following morning (2300–0700); off duty watch. J.T.E.*

in murder. The idea behind this arrangement was that, if death should result from the commission of any of those crimes, the investigating officers would have some prior knowledge of the events which lead up to it. Furthermore, unlike the officers of the G.C.P.D., whose authority ended at the city limits, the deputies had jurisdiction throughout the whole of Rockabye County.[9]

9. *Such an arrangement has long been accepted practise in the United States of America. In the days of the 'Old West', municipal officers such as constables, town marshals and their deputies, etc., only had jurisdictional authority within the limits of the village, town, or city, which employed them. Members of the sheriff's office were similarly restricted to operating within the boundaries of the county (parish in Louisiana). As is the case with present day State Police and the Highway Patrol, the Texas and Arizona Rangers could cover the whole of the State by whom they were formed. U.S. Marshals and members of the Federal Bureau of Investigation have jurisdiction everywhere in the United States of America, but their investigations are generally restricted to major, or 'Federal' offenses such as kidnapping, hijacking of aircraft, or robberies of U.S. post offices or mail. J.T.E.*

Appendix Two

Unlike her partner, Deputy Sheriff Bradford 'Brad' Counter, *q.v.,* Woman Deputy Alice Fayde had entered the Rockabye County Sheriff's Office by the conventional means. Prior to having 'caught her star', she had served for seven years as a member of the Gusher City Police Department's Bureau of Women Officers. Rising through the ranks, from walking a beat to becoming a sergeant in the Detective Bureau, she had gained experience by working out of such diverse Divisions as Evans Hill — the low rent area known to the local law enforcement agencies and its residents as 'the Bad Bit' — and the elite, high rent, Upton Heights. On winning her promotion to the Detective Bureau, she had added to her practical knowledge by serving with various specialist departments such as Traffic, Juvenile, Vice & Gambling and Narcotics.

Joining Brad to help bring to justice the professional killers who had murdered her uncle, Deputy Sheriff Thomas Cord. Alice had become the permanent partner of the blond giant. Without in any way affecting their ability to function as a team, their association became much closer as time went by.[1] By virtue of her greater length of service and practical 'street' experience, she was the senior member of the team and Brad had not the slightest objection to the arrangement.

Alice possessed a sound knowledge of self defense,

1. *How the change in the association came about is told in:* THE ¼ SECOND DRAW. *J.T.E.*

being well able to protect herself when necessary in bare handed combat against other women.[2] In addition, she was skilled in the use of firearms and her ability with a handgun had given her a classification of Expert, for which she received an increment of eight dollars a week to her salary.[3] Although at the time of this narrative she was carrying a Colt Cobra .38 Special revolver with a two and a half inch barrel, having seen a demonstration of its lack of penetrative powers, she later changed to a Colt Commander .45 automatic pistol — a lightweight version of the Colt Government Model of 1911 — which was vastly more potent than her previous choice.[4]

2. *Four occasions on which Woman Deputy Alice Fayde needed to make use of her knowledge of unarmed combat when in contention against other women are described in:* THE SHERIFF OF ROCKABYE COUNTY; THE PROFESSIONAL KILLERS — *which also covers the investigation into the murder of Deputy Sheriff Thomas Cord* — THE DEPUTIES *and* BAD HOMBRE. *J.T.E.*

3. *One occasion when Woman Deputy Alice Fayde was compelled to put her ability with a handgun to serious use is described in:* Part Three, 'A Contract For Alice Fayde', J.T.'S LADIES. *J.T.E.*

4. *The incident which led to the change of armament for Woman Deputy Alice Fayde is to be found in the volume to which we refer in* Footnote One *above. J.T.E.*

Appendix Three
Radio Codes

353a	*Escape From Jail*
450	*Unlawful Assembly To Frighten Anyone By Disguise*
454a	*Wearing Mask In Public*
474	*Disturbing The Peace*
477	*Drunk In Public Place*
483	*Unlawfully Carrying Firearms*
489b	*Possession Or Sale, Etc., Of Machine Guns*
490	*Bigamy*
525	*Procuring For Immoral Purposes*
535c	*Indecent Exposure To Child*
625	*Keeping Premises For Gambling Purposes*
666–4	*Manufacture, Sale Or Possession Of Liquor Unlawful (Moonshining)*
725b	*Violation Of Narcotics Laws*
725d	*Transportation Or Possession Of Contraband Narcotics*
1148	*Aggravated Assault*
1151	*Assault With A Prohibited Weapon*
1160	*Assault With Intent To Murder*
1162	*Assault With Intent To Rape*
1164	*Assault In Attempting Robbery*
1189	*Rape*
1256	*Murder*
1265	*Seriously Threatening Life*
1314	*Arson (Private Property)*
1397	*Burglary*
1398	*Burglary Employing Explosives*

1408	*Robbery*
1440	*Theft Of Horse Or Mule*
1441	*Theft Of Cow Or Hog*

The above are the numbers of the appropriate Articles of the Texas Penal Code

* * *

Code 1	— *Acknowledge Message*
Code 2	— *Urgent (No Red Light, Siren)*
Code 3	— *Emergency (Red Light, Siren)*
Code 4	— *No Further Help Needed*
Code 4 (Adam)	— *Sufficient Help At The Scene; Suspect Still In Vicinity*
Code 6 (Adam)	*Out For Investigation, May Need Assistance*
Code 7	— *Off Watch To Eat*
Code 8	— *Fire Alarm Box Pulled*
Code 9	— *Request For Assistance*
Code 20	— *Notify News Photographers*
A.C.	*Aircraft Crash*
1020	*What Is Your Location?*
10−4	*Message Understood?*
Roger	*Understood*

* * *

MAJOR DISASTER

| Code 12 | — *Disaster is believed present. Field Units to reconnoitre their beats and report evidence of damage. Off duty officers and reserves notified. Stand by for one hour for instructions.* |
| Code 13 (Fred) | *Disaster has occurred. Field Units reconnoitre their beats and report extent of damage. Off duty officers and reserves notified. Report as planned. Suffix will indicate area affected.* |

Code 13 (Daniel)	*Disaster has occurred. Field Units reconnoitre their beats and report extent of damage. All off duty officers, reserves and auxiliaries report as planned.*
Code 14	*Recall Code 12 and/or Code 13 in its every form. All officers return to normal duties. Reserves and auxiliaries relieved of further duties.*

*   *   *

The employment of code numbers is less of a security measure, against criminals monitoring the calls, than a means by which the Dispatchers of the Bureau Of Communications' Central Control can pass information quickly to the officers on patrol.

Appendix Four

Before questioning a suspect, a peace officer in Rockabye County is required to carry out the following procedure by saying:

'In keeping with the Supreme Court's decision in "Miranda versus Arizona", I am not permitted to ask you any questions until you have been warned of your right to counsel and your privilege against self incrimination.

First; you have the right to remain silent if you choose.

Second; you do not have to answer questions asked by myself or any other peace officer if you don't want to.

Third; if you decide to answer any questions, the answers may be used against you.

You also have the right to consult with an attorney before, or during, questioning.

If you do not have the money to hire a lawyer, one will be appointed to consult with you.'

Between each sentence, the officer has to ask whether the suspect understands what it means. Should the suspect be of an ethnic origin which does not claim English as its first tongue, an interpreter must be produced to 'read the rights' in the appropriate language. If this is not done, they may be ruled invalid on a claim they were not understood

If you have enjoyed reading this book and other works by the same author, why not join

THE J. T. EDSON APPRECIATION SOCIETY

You will receive a signed photograph of J. T. Edson, bi-monthly Newsletters giving details of all new books and re-prints of earlier titles.

Competitions with autographed prizes to be won in every issue of the Edson Newsletter.

A chance to meet J. T. Edson.

Send S.A.E. for details and membership form to:

The Secretary,
J. T. Edson Appreciation Society,
P.O. Box 13,
MELTON MOWBRAY,
Leics.

YOU'RE A TEXAS RANGER, ALVIN FOG
by J. T. Edson

In every democracy the laws for the protection of the innocent allows loopholes through which the guilty can slip. . . .
The Govenor of Texas decided that only unconventional
methods could cope with the malefactors who slipped
through the meshes of the law and so was formed a select
group of Texas Rangers. Picked for their courage, honesty,
and devotion to justice, they were known as Company
Z. . . .

With one exception every man in Company Z had been a
member of the Texas Rangers for several years. Alvin Fog
was that man. He had inherited the muscle, skill at gun
handling and bare handed fighting of his grandfather, the
legendary Rio Hondo gun wizard, Dusty Fog. But still his
fellows in Company Z were not convinced he had the skill
needed for their unconventional duties. It was up to him to
prove he was worthy of his place in Company Z. He alone
could make his fellow rangers say. . . . 'You're a Texas
Ranger, Alvin Fog. . . .'

0 552 11177 5   75p

A SELECTION OF J. T. EDSON WESTERNS
THAT APPEAR IN CORGI

ORDER FORM

All these books are available at your book shop or newsagent, or can be ordered direct from the publisher. Just tick the titles you want and fill in the form below.

CORGI BOOKS, Cash Sales Department, P.O. Box 11, Falmouth, Cornwall.

Please send cheque or postal order, no currency.

Please allow cost of book(s) plus the following for postage and packing:

U.K. Customers—Allow 45p for the first book, 20p for the second book and 14p for each additional book ordered, to a maximum charge of £1.63.

B.F.P.O. and Eire—Allow 45p for the first book, 20p for the second book plus 14p per copy for the next 7 books, thereafter 8p per book.

Overseas Customers—Allow 75p for the first book and 21p per copy for each additional book.

NAME (Block Letters) ....

ADDRESS ....

....